Three delightful animal stories about an owl, a cat and a hen by the ever-popular Jill Tomlinson. Perfect for snuggling down to a good read.

Also by Jill Tomlinson

The Aardvark Who Wasn't Sure
The Gorilla Who Wanted To Grow Up
The Otter Who Wanted To Know
The Penguin Who Wanted to Learn

THREE FAVOURITE ANIMAL STORIES

JILL TOMLINSON

Illustrated by Paul Howard

EGMONT

EGMONT

We bring stories to life

The Owl Who Was Afraid of the Dark
was first published in Great Britain 1968

The Cat Who Wanted to Go Home
was first published in Great Britain 1972

The Hen Who Wouldn't Give Up
was first published in Great Britain 1967 as *Hilda the Hen*
Published as *The Hen Who Wouldn't Give Up* 1977

Published in one volume as *Three Favourite Animal Stories* 2003
This edition published 2005
by Egmont Books Limited
239 Kensington High Street
London W8 6SA

ISBN 1 4052 2009 0

1 3 5 7 9 10 8 6 4 2

A CIP catalogue record for this title is available from the British Library

Printed and bound in Great Britain by the CPI Group

Contents

The
Owl
Who Was
Afraid of
the Dark

For Philip and, of course, D. H.

Contents

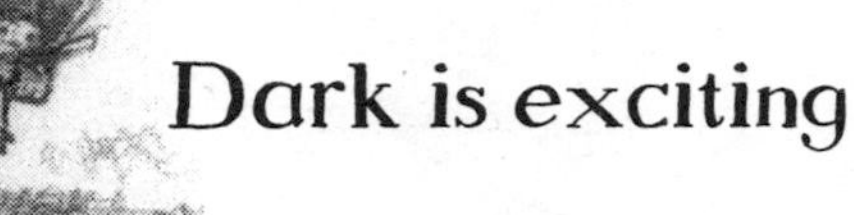

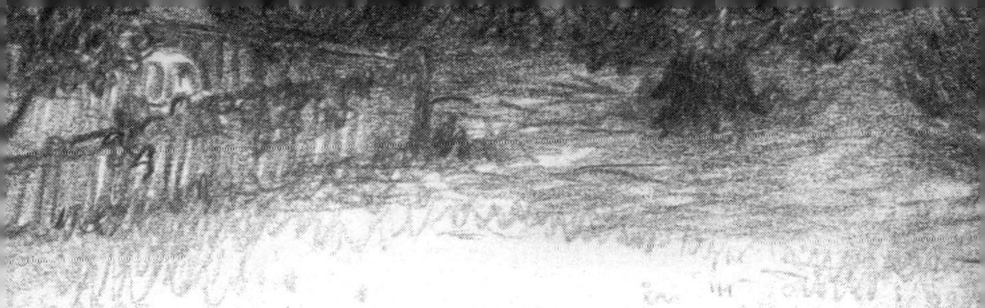

Dark is exciting

Plop was a baby barn owl, and he lived with his mummy and daddy at the top of a very tall tree in a field.

Plop was fat and fluffy.

He had a beautiful heart-shaped ruff.

He had enormous, round eyes.

He had very knackety knees.

In fact he was exactly the same as every baby barn owl that has ever been – except for one thing.

Plop was afraid of the dark.

'You *can't* be afraid of the dark,' said his mummy. 'Owls are *never* afraid of the dark.'

'This one is,' Plop said.

'But owls are *night* birds,' she said.

Plop looked down at his toes. 'I don't want to be a night bird,' he mumbled. 'I want to be a day bird.'

'You *are* what you *are*,' said Mrs Barn Owl firmly.

'Yes, I know,' agreed Plop, 'and what I are is afraid of the dark.'

'Oh dear,' said Mrs Barn Owl. It was clear that she was going to need a lot of patience. She shut her eyes and tried to think how best she could help Plop not to be afraid. Plop waited.

His mother opened her eyes again. ‘Plop, you are only afraid of the dark because you don’t know about it. What *do* you know about the dark?’

‘It’s black,’ said Plop.

‘Well, that’s wrong for a start. It can be silver or blue or grey or lots of other colours, but almost never black. What else do you know about it?’

‘I don’t like it,’ said Plop. ‘I do not like it AT ALL.’

‘That’s not *knowing* something,’ said his mother. ‘That’s *feeling* something. I don’t think you know anything about the dark at all.’

‘Dark is nasty,’ Plop said loudly.

'You don't know that. You have never had your beak outside the nest-hole after dusk. I think you had better go down into the world and find out a lot more about the dark before you make up your mind about it.'

'Now?' said Plop.

'Now,' said his mother.

Plop climbed out of the nest-hole and wobbled along the branch outside. He peeped over the edge. The world seemed to be a very long way down.

'I'm not a very good lander,' he said. 'I might spill myself.'

'Your landing will improve with practice,' said his mother. 'Look! There's a little boy down there on the edge of the wood collecting sticks. Go and talk to him about it.'

'Now?' said Plop.

'Now,' said his mother. So Plop shut his eyes, took a deep breath, and fell off his branch.

His small white wings carried him down but, as he said, he was not a good lander. He did seven very fast somersaults past the little boy.

'Ooh!' cried the little boy. 'A giant Catherine-wheel!'

'Actually,' said the Catherine-wheel, picking himself up, 'I'm a barn owl.'

'Oh yes – so you are,' said the little boy with obvious disappointment. 'Of course, you couldn't be a firework yet. Dad says we can't have the fireworks until it gets dark. Oh, I wish it would hurry up and get dark *soon*.'

'You *want* it to get dark?' said Plop in amazement.

'Oh, YES,' said the little boy. 'DARK IS EXCITING. And tonight is specially exciting because we're going to have fireworks.'

'What are fireworks?' asked Plop. 'I don't think owls have them – not barn owls, anyway.'

'Don't you?' said the little boy. 'Oh, you poor thing. Well, there are rockets, and flying saucers, and volcanoes, and golden rain, and sparklers, and . . .'

'But what *are* they?' begged Plop. 'Do you eat them?'

'NO!' laughed the little boy. 'Daddy sets fire to their tails and they *whoosh* into the air and fill the sky with coloured stars – well, the rockets, that is. I'm allowed to hold the sparklers.'

'What about the volcanoes? And the golden rain? What do they do?'

'Oh, they sort of burst into showers of stars. The golden rain *pours* – well, like rain.'

'And the flying saucers?'

'Oh, they're super! They whizz round your head and make a sort of *wheeee* noise. I like them best.'

'I think I would like fireworks,' said Plop.

'I'm sure you would,' the little boy said. 'Look here, where do you live?'

'Up in that tree – in the top flat. There are squirrels farther down.'

'That big tree in the middle of the field? Well, you can watch our fireworks from there! That's our garden – the one with the swing. You look out as soon as it gets dark . . .'

'Does it *have* to be dark?' asked Plop.

'Of course it does! You can't see fireworks unless it's dark. Well, I must go. These sticks are for the bonfire.'

'Bonfire?' said Plop. 'What's that?'

'You'll see if you look out tonight. Goodbye!'

'Goodbye,' said Plop, bobbing up and down in a funny little bow.

He watched the boy run across the field, and then took a little run himself, spread his wings, and fluttered up to the landing branch.

He slithered along it on his tummy and dived head first into the nest-hole.

'Well?' said his mother.

'The little boy says DARK IS EXCITING.'

'And what do you think, Plop?'

'I still do not like it AT ALL,' said Plop, 'but I'm going to watch the fireworks – if you will sit by me.'

'I will sit by you,' said his mother.

'So will I,' said his father, who had just woken up. 'I like fireworks.'

So that is what they did.

When it began to get dark, Plop waddled to the mouth of the nest-hole and peered out cautiously.

'Come on, Plop! I think they're starting,' called Mr Barn Owl. He was already in position on a big branch at the very top of the tree. 'We shall see beautifully from here.'

Plop took two brave little steps out of the nest-hole.

'I'm here,' said his mother quietly. 'Come on.'

So together, wings almost touching, they flew up to join Mr Barn Owl.

They were only just in time. There were flames leaping and crackling at the end of the little boy's garden. 'That must be the bonfire!' squeaked Plop.

Hardly had Plop got his wings tucked away, when '*WHOOSH!*' – up went a rocket and spat out a shower of green stars. 'Ooooh!' said Plop, his eyes like saucers.

A fountain of dancing stars sprang up from the ground – and another and another.

Ooooh!' said Plop again.

'You sound like a Tawny owl,' said his father. 'Goodness! What's that?'

Something was whizzing about leaving bright trails of squiggles behind it and making a loud 'Wheeee!' noise.

'Oh, that's a flying saucer,' said Plop.

'Really?' his father said. 'I've never seen one of those before. You seem to know all about it. What's that fizzy one that keeps jigging up and down?'

'I expect that's my friend with a sparkler. Oooooh! There's a me!'

'I beg your pardon?' said Plop's father.

'It's a Catherine-wheel! The little boy thought I was a Catherine-wheel when I landed. Oh, isn't it beautiful? And he thought *I* was one!'

Mr Barn Owl watched the whirling, sparking circles spinning round and round.

'That must have been quite a landing!' he said.

Dark is kind

When the very last firework had faded away, Mr Barn Owl turned to Plop.

'Well, son,' he said. 'I'm off hunting now. Would you like to come?'

Plop looked at the darkness all around them. It seemed even blacker after the bright fireworks. 'Er – not this time, thank you, Daddy. I can't see; I've got stars in my eyes.'

'I see,' said his father. 'In that case I shall

have to go by myself.' He floated off into the darkness like a great white moth.

Plop turned in distress to his mother.

'I *wanted* to go with him. I *want* to like the dark. It's just that I don't seem to be able to.'

'You will be able to, Plop. I'm quite sure about that.'

'I'm not sure,' said Plop.

'Well, I *am*,' his mother said. 'Now, come on. You'd better have your rest. You were awake half the day.'

So Plop had his midnight rest, and when he woke up, his father was back with his dinner. Plop swallowed it in one huge gulp. 'That was nice,' he said. 'What was it?'

'A mouse,' said Mr Barn Owl.

'I like mouse,' said Plop. 'What's next?'

'I have no idea,' his father said. 'It's

Mummy's turn now. You'll have to wait till she gets back.'

Plop was always hungry, and his mother and father were kept very busy bringing him food all night long. When daylight came, they were very tired and just wanted to go to sleep.

'Bedtime, Plop,' said Mrs Barn Owl.

'I don't want to go to bed,' said Plop. 'I want to be a day bird.'

'Well, *I* am a night bird,' said his mother. 'And if your father and I don't get any sleep today, *you* won't get anything to eat tonight.'

Plop did not like the sound of that at all, so he drew himself up straight and tall – well, as tall as he could – and tried to go to sleep.

He did sleep for half the morning, but then he woke up full of beans – or perhaps it was mouse – and he just could not go back to sleep again.

He jiggled up and down on the branch where his poor parents were trying to roost. He practised standing on one leg, and taking off, and landing, and other important things that a little owl has to learn to do. Then he thought he would try out his voice. He tried to make a real, grown-up barn owl noise.

'EEeek!' he screeched. 'EEEEEK!'

It sounded like the noise a cat makes if you accidentally tread upon its tail. Plop was very pleased with it.

Mrs Barn Owl was not. She half opened one bleary eye. 'Plop, dear,' she said. 'Wouldn't you like to go down into the world again and find out some more about the dark?'

'Now?' said Plop.

'Now,' said his mother.

'Don't you want to hear my screech first? It's getting jolly good.'

'I heard it,' Mrs Barn Owl said. 'Look, there's an old lady in a deckchair down there in that garden. Go and disturb – I mean, go and find out what she thinks about the dark.'

So Plop shut his eyes, took a deep breath, and fell off his branch.

He did not get his wings working in time. He fell faster and faster and finally plunged at the old lady's feet with an earth-shaking thump.

'Gracious!' cried the old lady. 'A thunderbolt!'

'A-a-a-actually, I'm a barn owl,' said the thunderbolt when he had got his breath back.

'Really?' said the old lady, peering at Plop over the top of her glasses. 'I do beg your pardon. My eyes are not as good as they used to be. How nice of you to – er – drop in.'

'Well, it wasn't nice of me, exactly,' Plop said truthfully. 'I came to ask you about something.'

'Did you?' said the old lady. 'Now what could that be, I wonder?'

'I wanted to ask you about the dark. You see, I'm a bit afraid of it, and that's rather awkward for an owl. We're supposed to be night birds.'

'That is a problem,' said the old lady. 'Have you tried carrots?'

'What?'

'Don't say "what", say "I beg your pardon" if you don't hear the first time. I said, have you tried carrots? Wonderful things, carrots.'

'I don't think owls have carrots – not barn owls, anyway.'

'Oh. A pity. I've always sworn by carrots for helping one to see in the dark.'

'I *can* see in the dark,' said Plop. 'I can see for miles and miles.'

'Now, don't boast. It is not nice for little boys to boast.' The old lady leaned forward and peered closely at Plop.

'I suppose you are a little boy? It's so difficult to tell, these days. They all look the same.'

'Yes,' said Plop. 'I'm a boy owl, and I want to go hunting with Daddy, but he always goes hunting in the dark, and I'm afraid of it.'

'How very odd,' said the old lady. 'Now, I love the dark. I expect you will when you are my age. DARK IS KIND.'

'Tell me,' Plop said.

'*Please*,' said the old lady. 'Such a little word, but it works wonders.'

'Tell me, please,' said Plop obediently.

'Well, now,' the old lady began. 'Dark is kind in all sorts of ways. Dark hides things – like shabby furniture and the hole in the carpet. It hides my wrinkles and my gnarled old hands. I can forget that I'm old in the dark.'

'I don't think owls get wrinkles,' said Plop. 'Not barn owls, anyway. They just get a bit moth-eaten looking.'

'Don't interrupt!' said the old lady. 'It is very rude to interrupt. Where was I? Yes – dark is kind when you are old. I can sit in the dark and *remember*. I remember my dear husband, and my children when they were small, and all the good times we had together. I am never lonely in the dark.'

'I haven't much to remember, yet,' said Plop. 'I'm rather new, you see.'

'Dark is quiet, too,' said the old lady, looking hard at Plop. 'Dark is restful – unlike a little owl I know.'

'Me?' said Plop.

'You,' said the old lady. 'When I was a little girl, children were seen but not heard.'

'I'm not children,' said Plop. 'I'm a barn owl.'

'Same thing,' said the old lady. 'You remind me very much of my son William when he was about four. He had the same knackety knees.'

'Are my knees knackety?' asked Plop, squinting downwards. 'I can't see them. My tummy gets in the way.'

'Very,' said the old lady, 'but I expect they'll straighten out in time. William's did. Now, I'm going indoors to have a little rest.'

Plop was surprised. 'I thought it was only owls who slept in the daytime,' he said. 'Are you a night bird, too?'

The old lady smiled. 'No, just an old bird. A very tired old bird.'

'Goodbye, then. I'll go now,' said Plop. 'Thank you for telling me about the dark.'

He fluttered up to the old lady's shoulder and nibbled her ear very gently.

The old lady was enchanted. 'An owl kiss!' she said. 'How very kind.'

Plop jumped down again and bobbed his

funny little bow.

'Such charming manners!' said the old lady.

Then Plop took a little run, spread his wings, and flew up to the landing branch.

'Well?' said his mother.

'The old lady says DARK IS KIND.'

'And what do you think, Plop?'

'I still do not like it AT ALL. Do you think my knees are knackety?'

'Of course,' said his mother. 'All little barn owls have knackety knees.'

'Oh, good,' said Plop. 'And what do you think the old lady said? She said children should be seen but not heard!'

Mr Barn Owl opened one sleepy eye.

'Hear! Hear!' he said.

Dark is fun

That evening when it was getting dark, Mr Barn Owl invited Plop to go hunting with him again. 'Coming, son?' he said. 'It's a lovely night.'

'Er – not this time, thank you, Daddy,' said Plop, who was sitting just outside the nest-hole. 'I'm busy.'

'You don't look busy,' Mr Barn Owl said. 'What are you doing?'

'I am busy *remembering*,' said Plop.

'I see,' said his father. 'In that case I shall have to go by myself.' He swooped off into the darkness like a great, silent jet aeroplane.

'What are you remembering, Plop?' asked his mother.

'I'm remembering what the old lady said about dark being kind. She says she is never lonely in the dark because she has so much to remember.'

'Well then,' said Mrs Barn Owl, 'this would seem to be a good moment for me to slip out and do a little hunting.'

'You're not going to leave me by myself!' said Plop.

'I shan't be very long. I'll try to bring you back something nice.'

'But I shall be lonely.'

'No, you won't. You just keep busy remembering like the old lady said.'

Plop watched his mother float off into the darkness like a white feather. The darkness seemed to come towards him and wrap itself around him.

'Dark is kind,' Plop muttered to himself. 'Dark is kind. Oh dear, what shall I remember?' He closed his eyes and tried to remember something to remember. Fireworks! He would remember the fireworks. He had enjoyed them. The darkness had been spotted and striped and sploshed with coloured lights above the glow of the bonfire. He still had stars in his eyes when he thought of it.

Shouts – happy shouts – from under his tree brought Plop back from his remembering. He opened his eyes and peered down through the leaves. There were people running about in his field, and flames were flickering from a pile of sticks. Another bonfire! Did that mean more fireworks?

Plop watched excitedly. He could see now that the people running about were boys – quite big boys in shorts. They were collecting more wood for the fire.

Suddenly they all disappeared into the woods with squeals and yells. All but one, that is. There was one boy left, sitting on a log near the fire.

Plop forgot about being afraid of the dark. He had to know what was going on. So he shut his eyes, took a deep breath, and fell off his branch.

The ground was nearer than he expected it to be, and he landed with an enormous thud.

'Coo!' said the boy on the log. 'A roly-poly pudding! Who threw that?'

'Nobody threw me – I just came,' said the roly-poly pudding, 'and actually I'm a barn owl.'

'So you are,' said the boy. 'Have you fallen out of your nest?'

Plop drew imself up as tall as he could. 'I did not fall – I flew,' he said. 'I'm just not a very good lander, that's all. I came to see if you were going to have fireworks, as a matter of fact.'

'Fireworks?' said the boy. 'No. What made you think that?'

'Well, the bonfire,' Plop said.

'Bonfire!' said the boy. 'This is no *bonfire*! This is a camp-fire – and I'm guarding it till the others get back.'

'Where have they gone?' asked Plop.

'They've gone to play games in the dark, lucky things.'

'Do you *like* playing games in the dark?' asked Plop.

'It's super!' said the boy. 'DARK IS FUN. Even quite ordinary games like Hide-and-Seek are fun in the dark. My favourite is the game where one of you stands outside a "home" with a torch in his hand, and shines it on anything he sees or hears moving. The rest of you have to creep past him and "home" without being spotted. It's super!'

There was a crash, and a yell of 'Scumbo! Got you!' from the wood.

'There – they're playing it now. Old Scumbo always gets caught first. He's got such big feet. You have to creep like a shadow not to be caught. Oh, it *would* be my turn to guard the fire.'

'What's the fire for?' asked Plop.

'Well, we cook potatoes in it, and make cocoa, and sing round it.'

'What for?'

'What for? Because it's fun, that's why, and because Boy Scouts have always had camp-fires.'

'Is that what you are? A Boy Scout?'

'Of course, silly, or I wouldn't be here, would I? I must put some more wood on the fire.'

Plop watched the Boy Scout build up the fire. 'Could – could I be a Boy Scout, do you think?' he asked.

'I doubt it,' said the Scout. 'You're a bit on the small side. I suppose you could be a Cub, but you have to be eight years old.'

'I'm eight weeks,' said Plop.

'Looks as if you'll have a long wait, then, doesn't it?' said the Scout. 'Anyway,' – he grinned – 'you'd look jolly silly in the uniform!'

Plop looked so disappointed that the Scout added, 'Never mind. You can stay for the sing-song tonight.'

'Oh, can I!' cried Plop. 'That would be soo – super!'

'You'd better go home and ask your mother first, though.'

So Plop flew up to the nest-hole – and found his mother waiting.

'Where have you been?' she said. She

sounded a bit cross, like all mothers when they have been worried.

'I've been talking to a Boy Scout, and he says DARK IS FUN, and he says I can stay for the camp-fire, so can I, Mummy, please?'

'Well, yes, all right,' she said.

'Oh, super!' said Plop.

So Plop was a Boy Scout for a night. He sat on his new friend's shoulder and was introduced to all the others. They made a great fuss of him and he had a wonderful time. He did not care for cocoa, but he enjoyed a small potato. His friend blew on it for him to cool it, because he knew that owls swallow their food whole, and a hot potato in the tummy would have been very uncomfortable for Plop!

The Scouts huddled round the fire and

sang and sang while the sparks danced. They sang funny songs and sad songs, long songs and short songs. Plop did not sing because he wanted to listen, but every now and then he got a bit excited and fluttered round the boys' heads crying 'Eeek! Eeeek!' and everybody laughed.

They sang until the fire had sunk to a deep, red glow and Plop had turned quite pink in its light.

Then it was time to go home, for the boys and for Plop. And when Plop had said goodbye to them all, and bowed and bowed till he ached, he spread his wings and flew up to the landing branch.

'Well?' said his mother.

'I told you. The Boy Scout says DARK IS FUN.'

'And what do you think, Plop?'

'I still do not like it AT ALL – but I think camp-fires are super! Did you bring me something special?'

'I did.'

Plop swallowed it in one gulp.

'That was nice,' he said. 'What was it?'

'A grasshopper.'

'I like grasshopper,' said Plop. 'What's next?'

Dark is necessary

Plop asked 'What's next' a great many times during that night. He sat just outside the nest-hole making loud snoring noises. He was not asleep – just hungry. Owls always snore when they're hungry.

'Oh, Plop. I shall be glad when you can hunt for yourself,' said Mrs Barn Owl wearily when Plop had gulped down his seventh – or was it his eighth? – dinner.

'What's next?' asked Plop.

'Nothing,' said his mother. 'You can't possibly have room for anything else.'

'I have,' said Plop. 'My mouse place is full up, but my grasshopper place isn't.'

'That's just too bad,' said Mrs Barn Owl, stretching and settling herself down to roost.

Mr Barn Owl swooped in, clapping his wings. He dropped something at Plop's feet. Plop swallowed it in one gulp. It was deliciously slippery.

'That was nice,' he said. 'What was it?'

'A fish,' said his father.

'I like fish,' said Plop. 'What's next?'

'Bed,' said Mr Barn Owl. He kissed his wife goodnight – or good day, I suppose it was – and settled himself to roost.

Plop made a few hopeful snoring noises,

but it was clear that the feast was over. He wobbled into the nest-hole and was soon fast asleep himself.

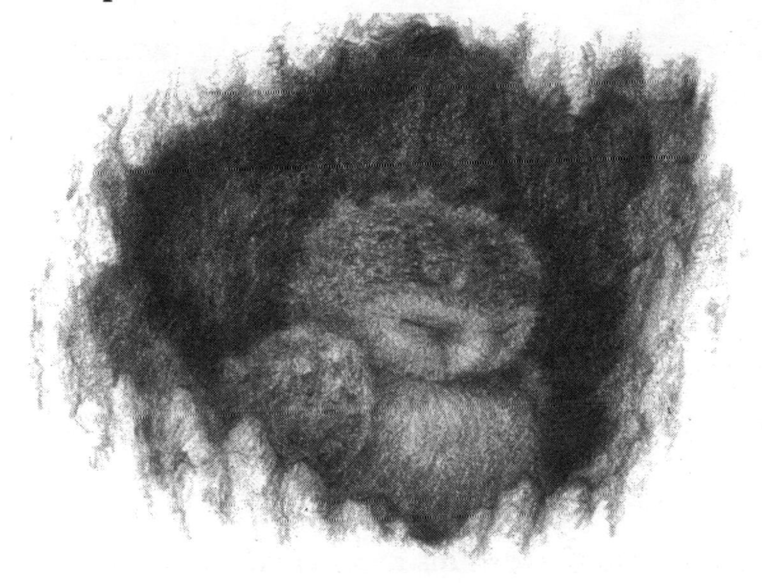

It was well into the afternoon when he woke up. He came out on to the landing branch and looked around. His parents were still drawn up as still as carvings, but the squirrels from downstairs were chasing each other up and down the trunk, their tails flying behind them. Plop watched them for a bit. One of them scuttled along the branch just below Plop's and then stopped abruptly and began to wash his face. He did not know that Plop was there – after all, owls are *supposed* to be asleep during the daytime.

Plop could not resist it. He bent down through the leaves and let out his very loudest 'Eeeek!'

The squirrel jumped into the air like a

jack-in-a-box, his ears a-quiver and his eyes like marbles. He flashed down the trunk and vanished into his hole.

Plop jumped up and down with delight. But of course he had done it again: he had woken his mother.

'Plop!'

'Yes, Mummy?'

'Go and find out some more about the dark, please, dear.'

'Now?' said Plop.

'Now,' said his mother. 'Go and ask that little girl what she thinks about it.'

'What little girl?'

'That little girl sitting down there – the one with the pony-tail.'

'Little girls don't have *tails*.'

'This one does. Go on now or you'll miss her.'

So Plop shut his eyes, took a deep breath, and fell off his branch.

His landing was a little better than usual. He bounced three times and rolled gently towards the little girl's feet.

'Oh! A woolly ball!' cried the little girl.

'Actually I'm a barn owl,' said the woolly ball.

'An owl? Are you sure?' she said, putting out a grubby finger and prodding Plop's round fluffy tummy.

'Quite sure,' said Plop, backing away and drawing himself up tall.

'Well, there's no need to be huffy,' said the little girl. 'You bounced. You must expect to be mistaken for a ball if you will go bouncing about the place. I've never met an owl before. Do you say "Tu-whit-a-woo"?'

'No,' said Plop. 'That's Tawny Owls.'

'Oh, you can't be a proper owl, then,' said the little girl. '*Proper* owls say "Tu-whit-a-woo"!'

'I *am* a proper owl!' said Plop, getting very cross. 'I am a barn owl, and barn owls go *Eeeek* like that.'

'Oh, don't *do* that!' said the little girl, putting her hands over her ears.

'Well, you shouldn't have made me cross,' said Plop. 'Anyway – *you* can't be a proper girl.'

'*What* did you say?' said the little girl, taking her hands off her ears.

'I said you're not a proper girl. Girls don't have *tails*. Squirrels have tails, rabbits have tails, mice . . .'

'This is a *pony*-tail,' said the little girl. 'It's the longest one in the class,' she added proudly.

'But why do you want to look like a pony?' asked Plop.

'Because – oh, because it's the fashion,' said the little girl. 'Don't you know *anything*?'

'Not much,' agreed Plop. 'Mummy says that that is why I'm afraid of the dark – because I don't know anything about it. Do *you* like the dark?'

The little girl looked at Plop in surprise. 'Well, of course I do,' she said. 'There has to be dark. DARK IS NECESSARY.'

'Dark is nessessess – is whatter?'

'Necessary. We need it. We can't do without it.'

'I could do without it,' said Plop. 'I could do without it very nicely.'

'Father Christmas wouldn't come,' said the little girl. 'You'll have an empty stocking on Christmas day.'

'I don't wear stockings,' said Plop, 'and who is Father Christmas?'

'Well, Father Christmas is a fat, jolly old man with a white beard, and he wears a red suit with a matching hat, and black boots.'

'Is that the fashion?' asked Plop.

'No,' said the little girl. 'It's just what he always wears in pictures of him – although I don't know how anybody knows because nobody has ever seen him.'

'What?' said Plop.

'Well, that's what I'm trying to tell you. *Father Christmas only comes in the dark*. He comes in the middle of the night, riding through the sky on a sledge pulled by reindeer.'

'Deer?' asked Plop. 'In the sky?'

'Magic deer,' said the little girl. 'Everything about Father Christmas is magic. Otherwise he couldn't possibly get round to all the children in the world in one night – or have enough toys for them all in his sack.'

'You didn't tell me about his sack.'

'He has a sack full of toys and he puts

them in the children's stockings.'

'In their stockings?' said Plop. 'With their feet in them? There can't be much room –'

'No, silly. We hang empty stockings at the ends of our beds for him to fill. I usually borrow one of Mummy's, but last year I hung up my tights.'

'And did he fill them?' breathed Plop.

'No – only one leg, but he did put a sugar mouse in the other one.'

'I'd rather have had a real mouse,' said Plop.

'So would I, really,' said the little girl. 'I wanted a white mouse, but Mummy says that if a mouse comes into the house she will leave it, and I suppose Father Christmas didn't want me to be an orphan.'

Plop was thinking. 'I don't think owls

have Father Christmas – not barn owls, anyway – and I haven't got a stocking to hang up.'

'Aah, what a shame,' said the little girl. 'Everybody should have Father Christmas. It's so exciting waking up in the morning and feeling all the bumps in your stocking and trying to guess what is in it.'

'Oh, stop it,' wailed Plop. 'I wish he would come to me.'

'Shut your eyes,' the little girl said. 'Go on. Shut them and you may get a surprise.'

Plop shut his eyes tight and waited. The little girl quickly pulled off her wellington and took off a sock. She was wearing two pairs because the boots were a bit big for her.

'Open your eyes!' she said to Plop, holding up the sock while she stood on one leg and wriggled her foot back into her wellington.

Plop opened his eyes – and then shut them again because he couldn't believe what he saw.

'Don't you want it?' said the little girl. 'I know it's a bit holey, but I don't expect Father Christmas will mind.'

'Oh, thank you,' said Plop, taking it with his beak and then holding it in his foot. 'Thank you *very* much. I'll go and hang it up at once.'

'Not yet,' laughed the little girl. 'You'll have to wait until Christmas Eve. Well, I must go now. It must be nearly tea-time. Goodbye. I do hope Father Christmas will come to you.'

'Goodbye,' said Plop, bobbing his funny little bow. 'You are very kind. You are a proper girl.'

'And you have a very nice "Eeek"!' said the little girl. 'I'm going to practise it to make my brothers jump. EEEK!' She ran off, and Plop could hear her 'eeeking' right across the field.

Plop picked up the sock in his beak, and flew up to the landing branch.

'Well?' said his mother.

'Jah lijjle yirl shays –' he began with his mouth full of sock. He put it down and tried again. 'The little girl says DARK IS NECESSARY, because of Father Christmas coming,' he said.

'And what do you think, Plop?'

'I still do not like it AT ALL – but I'm going to hang up this sock on Christmas Eve.'

And Plop took his sock and put it away very carefully in a corner of the nest-hole ready for Christmas.

Dark is fascinating

Plop, having slept nearly all day, was very lively that evening – very lively and very hungry. He kept wobbling along the branch to where his father was roosting to see if by chance he were awake and ready to go hunting.

Mr Barn Owl was drawn up tall and still. He seemed hardly to be breathing. Plop stretched up on tiptoe and tried to see into his father's face. What a strong, curved beak he had.

'Daddy, are you awake?' he said loudly. 'I'm hungry.'

Mr Barn Owl did not open his eyes, but the beak moved.

'Go away!' it said. 'I'm asleep.'

Plop went away obediently – and then realised something and went back again. 'Daddy! You can't be asleep. You spoke – I heard you.'

'You must have imagined it,' said his father, still not opening his eyes.

'You spoke,' said Plop. 'You're awake, so you can go hunting.' He butted his father's tummy with his head. 'Come on! It's getting-up time!'

Mr Barn Owl sighed and stretched.

'All right, all right, you horrible owlet. What time is it?' He looked up at the sky. 'Suffering bats! It isn't even dark yet! I could have had another half hour.' He glared at Plop. 'Dash it, I'm going to have another half hour. I will not be bullied by an addled little – little DAY BIRD. Go away! You may wake me when it is dark, and not before, d'you understand?' He suddenly leaned forward until his huge beak was level with Plop's own little carpet tack. Plop could see two of himself reflected in his father's eyes.

'Er – yes, Daddy,' he said, backing away hurriedly.

'Good,' said his father, drawing himself up to sleep again. 'Good day.'

Plop went back to the nest-hole to complain to his mother. A sleepy Mrs Barn

Owl listened sympathetically.

'Well, dear, I should go and find out some more about the world if I were you,' she said. 'Look! There's a young lady down there. Why don't you go and talk to her?'

Plop peered down through the leaves.

Standing a little way from the tree was someone wearing shiny black boots, a bright red fur coat with a matching hat, and what looked like a white beard.

'That's not a young lady!' shrieked Plop. 'That's Father Christmas!'

And he fell off his branch in such a hurry that he forgot either to shut his eyes *or* to take a deep breath.

He landed quite well, considering, but lost his balance at the last moment and toppled forward on to his face.

A gentle hand picked him up and set him right way up again.

'Oh, you poor darling,' said a sweet young voice. 'Are you all right?'

Plop looked up quickly. That voice didn't sound right.

It wasn't a white beard – it was long blond hair.

'You're not Father Christmas at all!' he said crossly. 'And I came down *specially*.'

'I'm terribly sorry,' said the young lady. 'And I'm not a darling. I'm a barn owl.'

'I tell you what,' the Father Christmas Lady said. 'May I draw a picture of you in my Nature Sketch Book? I haven't got a barn owl in it.'

'Me?' said Plop. 'You mean *really* me?'

'Yes, please. Perhaps you could pose on that low branch for me.'

Plop fluttered up to the branch and stood stiffly to attention. The Father Christmas Lady sat on a log and began to draw.

'I always carry my sketch book about with me in case I see something interesting,' she said.

The interesting barn owl drew himself up proudly like a soldier in a sentry box.

But not for long. The young lady looked

up from her drawing to find that her barn owl had completely disappeared.

'Can I see?' said a small voice down by her boot. Plop was jiggling up and down trying to see what was on the pad.

'There's not much to see, yet,' she said, 'but all right – you can look.'

Plop looked. 'I'm not bald like that!' he said indignantly.

'I haven't had time to get you properly dressed,' said the young lady.

'And you've only given me one leg.'

'I'm afraid a bald, one-legged barn owl is all there's going to be unless you keep still.'

Plop really tried very hard after that, and he only got down three or four times to see how she was getting on.

He could hardly believe his eyes when it

was finished. 'Is that really me?' he said. 'I look just like Daddy – well, almost.'

'Yes, that's really you,' she said. 'I keep one end of the book for animals and birds that come out in the daytime and the other end for night creatures. I've put you with them, of course.'

'Oh,' said Plop. 'Er – of course.'

'All the most interesting ones are your end,' the young lady went on. 'I think DARK IS FASCINATING.'

'I – er – *tell* me about it,' said Plop. (Well, it was too late now to tell her that she had got him at the wrong end of the book!)

'Hop up then,' said the young lady, holding out a finger and taking Plop on to her lap, 'and I'll show you what good company you are in. Look – here are some badgers.'

Plop looked at the big black and white animals with stripes down their noses. 'Funny faces they've got.'

'That's so they don't bump into each other in the dark,' explained the young lady. 'They can't see very well.'

She turned over the page. 'Ah! Now I think these are the most fascinating night creatures of all – bats.'

'You've got it the wrong way up,' said Plop.

The Father Christmas Lady laughed.

'No, I haven't. That's how bats like to be when they're not fluttering about – hanging upside down by their feet.'

'Go on!' said Plop.

'Yes, really. And do you know, if you were a baby bat your mother would take you with her wherever she went, clinging to her fur. You'd get lots of rides.'

'Oh, I'd like that,' Plop said.

'Yes, but when you got too big to be carried, do you know what your mother would do? She'd hang you up before she went out!'

'Hang me up?' said Plop. 'Upside down?'

'That's right. Now, let's see what else we can find.' She turned a few pages. 'Yes, here we are – oh!'

Plop was not with her.

He was rocking backwards and forwards on the low branch like one of those little wobbly men that you push. Every now and then he went a bit too far and had to waggle his wings to keep his balance.

'What are you doing?' asked the young lady.

'I'm trying to be a bat,' said Plop, 'but what I don't understand is how they begin. I can't *get* upside down.'

'Perhaps it would be easier to be a hedgehog,' said the young lady. 'When they're frightened they roll themselves into a ball, look – here's a picture of one.'

Plop hopped back on to her knee and inspected the hedgehog.

'His feathers could do with a bit of fluffing up,' he said.

'Those aren't feathers – they're prickles. Very useful they are, too. A hedgehog can jump off quite a high fence without hurting himself because he makes himself into a prickly ball and just bounces.'

'Very useful,' said Plop. 'I wish I had prickles.' He jumped off her lap and tried to roll himself into a ball.

It was very difficult. 'I don't seem to have enough bends,' he said.

Suddenly he stopped rolling about and stayed still, listening. Then he rushed back to the young lady's lap and tried to bury himself in her coat.

'What's the matter?' she said.

'THERE'S A FUNNY NOISE,' he said. 'OVER THERE.'

The young lady listened. There was a busy, rustling sound coming from the dry leaves under the big tree.

'Why, I do believe it's a hedgehog!' she said. 'Yes, here he is. Look!'

Plop peeped cautiously over the edge of her lap. A tiny pointed snout pushed its way through the leaves, and then a small round creature scuttled across the ground in front of them.

'They never bother to move about quietly,' the young lady whispered, 'because they know nobody would want to eat anything so prickly.'

'Is he sure?' said Plop. 'I'm so hungry I could eat anything!'

The hedgehog stopped dead and rolled himself into a tight little ball.

'He must have heard you,' the young lady said reproachfully. 'What a thing to say.'

'Well, it's true,' Plop said. 'I'm starving.'

'Oh, of course! You'll be going hunting with your parents now that it's getting dark, won't you? I was forgetting you're a night bird.'

The night bird looked down at his toes.

'Well, I won't keep you,' she went on, 'except – would you mind doing something for me before you go? I *would* like to hear you screech.'

Plop didn't mind at all. He stuck out his

chest and gave her the most enormous 'EEEEEEEK!' he could possibly manage.

'Gorgeous!' said the young lady.

Plop bobbed his funny little bow. Then he took off and circled round, 'eeking' for all he was worth. The young lady waved, and then with one final 'eeeek!' of farewell, Plop flew up to the landing branch.

'Well?' said his mother.

'The Father Christmas Lady – you were right, it was a lady – says DARK IS FASCINATING.'

'And what do you think, Plop?'

'I still do not like it AT ALL. But what do you think? The lady drew a picture of me.'

'Well, that's very special, isn't it? Nobody has ever put me in a picture.'

'*And* she says my screech is gorgeous.'

'She does, does she? I wondered what all that noise was about.'

'Where's Daddy?'

'Out hunting.'

'Oh, jolly good. I could eat a hedgehog!'

'I wouldn't recommend it,' said his mother.

Dark is wonderful

'That was nice,' said Plop when he had gulped down what his father had brought. 'What was it?'

'A shrew,' said his father.

'I like shrew,' said Plop. 'What's next?'

'A short pause,' said Mrs Barn Owl. 'Let your poor daddy get his breath back.'

'All right,' said Plop, 'but do hurry up, Daddy. Shrews are nice, but they're not very big, are they? This one feels very lonely all by itself at the bottom of my tummy. It needs company.'

'I don't believe there is a bottom to your tummy,' said his father. 'No matter how much I put into it, it is never full. Oh well, I suppose I had better go and hunt for something else to cast into the bottomless pit.'

'That's what fathers are for,' said Plop. 'Wouldn't you like to go hunting, too, Mummy? It would be a nice change for you.'

'Thank you very much,' said Mrs Barn Owl. 'What you really mean is that you won't have to wait so long between courses! But I will certainly go if you don't mind being left.'

'Why don't you come with us?' said his father. 'Then you wouldn't have to wait at all.'

Plop looked round at the creeping

darkness. 'Er – no, thank you, Daddy,' he said. 'I have some more remembering to do.'

'Right'o,' said Mr Barn Owl. 'Ready, dear?'

Plop's parents took off together side by side, their great white wings almost touching. Plop sat outside the nest-hole and watched them drift away into the darkness until they melted into each other and then disappeared altogether. It took quite a long time, because the stars were coming out and Plop could see a long way by their light with his owl's eyes.

He remembered what his mother had said about dark never being black. It certainly was not black tonight. It was more of a misty grey, and the sky was pricked all over with tiny stars.

'Drat!' said a voice from somewhere below Plop.

Plop started and peered down through the leaves. There was a man with some sort of contraption set up in front of him, standing there scowling up at the cloud which had hidden the moon. What was he doing?

Plop shut his eyes, took a deep breath, and fell off his branch.

He shot through the air like a white streak and landed with a soft bump.

'Heavens!' cried the man. 'A shooting star!'

'Actually, I'm a barn owl,' said the shooting star. 'What's that thing you've got there?'

'A telescope,' said the man. 'A barn owl,

did you say? Well, well. I thought you were a meteor. How do you do?'

'How do I do what?' asked Plop.

'Oh – you know what I mean. How are you?'

'Hungry,' said Plop. 'I thought you said I was a shooting star, not a meteor.'

'A meteor *is* a shooting star.'

'Oh,' said Plop. 'What is the television for?'

'Telescope. For looking at things like the stars and planets.'

'Ooh! Can I have a look, please?'

'Of course,' said the man, 'but it's not a very good night for it, I'm afraid. Too cloudy.'

'I don't like the dark very much,' said Plop.

'Really?' said the man. 'How very odd. You must miss such a lot. DARK IS WONDERFUL.'

'Tell me,' said Plop. 'Please.'

'I'll do better than that – I'll show you,' the man said. 'Come and put your eye – no, no! *This* end!'

Plop had jumped up, scuttled along the telescope, and was now peering backwards between his feet into the wrong end.

'I can't see anything,' he said.

'You surprise me,' said the man. 'Try this end.'

Plop wobbled back along the telescope and the man supported him on his wrist so that his eye was level with the eye-piece.

'Now can you see anything?'

'Oh yes,' said Plop. 'It makes everything come nearer, doesn't it? I can see a bright, bright star. That must be very near.'

'Yes – just fifty-four million, million miles

away, that's all.'

'Million, million –!' gasped Plop.

'Yes, that's Sirius, the Dog Star. You're quite right – it is one of the nearest.' Obviously million millions were nothing to the man with a telescope.

'Why is it called the Dog Star?' asked Plop.

'Because it belongs to Orion, the Great Hunter. Look! There he is. Can you see those three stars close together?'

Plop drew his head back from the telescope and blinked.

'Can I change eyes?' he said. 'This one's getting very tired.'

'Yes, of course. Now – see if you can find the Great Hunter.'

'He has three stars close together, did you say?'

'Yes – that's his belt.'

'And some fainter stars behind him?'

'Yes – that's his sword.'

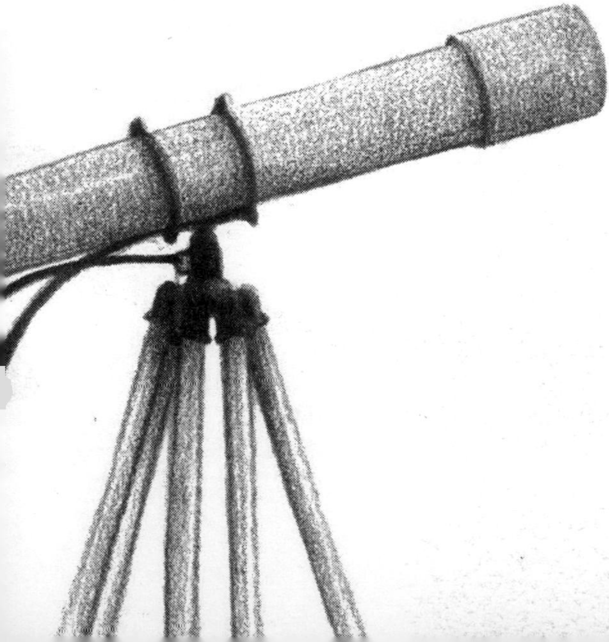

'I've got him!' shouted Plop. 'I've got Orion the Great Hunter. Oh, I never knew stars had names. Show me some more.'

'Well, we'll see if we can find the Pole Star, shall we? Hang on – I have to swing the telescope round for that.'

Plop had a ride on the telescope, and then the man showed him how to find the Plough and the two stars pointing straight up to the Pole Star. 'That's a bright one, too, isn't it?' said Plop.

'Yes. There! Now you can find that, you need never get lost, because that star is directly over the North Pole so you'll always know where north is.'

'Is that important?' asked Plop.

'Very important,' said the man. Heavens! What was that?' An eerie, long-drawn shriek had torn the peace of the night.

'Oh dear. I expect that's my daddy,' said Plop. They looked up. A ghostly, whitish form circled above them. 'Yes, it is. I'd better let him know I'm here. Eeeeeek!'

'Oh!' said the man, jumping. 'You should warn people when you're going to do that. You know, I've often wondered what that noise was. Now I shall know it is only you or your father.'

'Or my mother,' said Plop. 'I really must go. Thank you very, very much for teaching me about the stars.' He hopped on to the telescope and bowed his funny little bow. 'Goodbye.'

'Goodbye, Master Barn Owl. Good star-gazing!'

Plop flew up to join his father and

together they landed on the landing branch.

'Well?' said Plop's mother.

'The man with the telescope says DARK IS WONDERFUL, and he called me "Master Barn Owl" and . . .'

'And what do you think, Plop?'

'I know what *I* think,' said Mr Barn Owl, not giving Plop a chance to reply. 'I think Master Barn Owl has got a bit of a cheek to send his poor parents on an absolutely urgent search for food and then not bother to be in when they get back. I thought you were supposed to be starving?'

'I *am* starving,' said Plop, 'but did you know that the Dog Star is fifty-four million, million miles away . . .'

'Do you want your dinner or don't you?' said Mr Barn Owl.

'Oh yes,' said Plop. He gobbled down what his father had brought, and he gobbled down what his mother had brought, and not only did he not ask what it was that he had just eaten, but he did not even say 'What's next?'

What he said was, 'Daddy, do you know how to find the Pole Star? Shall I show you?'

'By all means,' said Mr Barn Owl, giving his wife a slow wink. 'Anything that can take your mind off your tummy like this *must* be worth seeing!'

Plop would not rest – and so neither could Mr and Mrs Barn Owl – until he had made quite sure that they could recognise all the stars which the man with the telescope had shown him.

He was still at it at about four o'clock in the morning.

'Now are you quite sure you understand about the Pole Star?' he said to his mother, who seemed to be being a bit dense about it.

'I think so, dear,' yawned Mrs Barn Owl. 'You find the thing that looks like a plough but is actually a big bear – or is it a small bear? – and the Pole Star is – um – near the North Star.'

'The Pole Star *is* the North Star,' Plop said impatiently, 'and the two stars at the front of the Plough point to it. I don't think you're really trying. You haven't been listening.'

'Oh, we have,' said Mr Barn Owl. 'We have been listening for hours and hours. I think perhaps Mummy is just a little bit tired . . .'

'But you must know how to find the Pole Star,' said Plop, 'or you might get lost.'

'I never get lost,' said his father indignantly, 'and neither does your mother. Now be a good chap and go into the nest-hole and I'll see if I can find you something nice for your supper. You can have it in bed for once, hmm?'

'Oh, all right,' said Plop, 'but I really do feel that you should know about these things. I'll have to try to explain again tomorrow.'

Mr Barn Owl turned to his wife in horror. 'Oh, no! Not tomorrow night as well! I couldn't stand it.'

'Never mind, dear,' said Mrs Barn Owl soothingly. 'You haven't had to do nearly as much hunting as usual.'

'I'm not at all sure that all this star-gazing isn't much more wearing than filling the bottomless pit!' groaned Mr Barn Owl.

'Oh, Daddy.' Plop put his head out of the nest-hole. 'Did I tell you about Orion? Orion is the Great Hunter and – oh, he's gone!'

'Yes, dear, he must finish his hunting before it gets light,' said his mother. 'Now you get back in there and mind you wash behind your ears properly. I'm coming to inspect you in a minute.'

So Plop had his supper in bed. And then, like a real night owl, he slept right through the daylight hours.

Dark is beautiful

When Plop woke up, it was already getting dark. He came out on to the landing branch. There was an exciting frosty nip in the air. 'Now who's a day bird!' Plop shouted at the darkness. 'I am what I am!'

'What *is* he bellowing about?' said Mr Barn Owl, waking up with a start.

'I believe Plop is beginning to enjoy being an owl at last,' said Mrs Barn Owl, 'but ssh! Pretend to be asleep.'

Plop waddled up to inspect them. They were drawn up tall. Fancy sleeping on such a lovely night! Well, he wasn't going to hang about waiting for them. He might be missing something. The man with a telescope might be back, or some Boy Scouts, or anything. He was going down to see.

So Plop shut his eyes, took a deep breath, and fell off his branch.

He floated down on his little white wings and landed like a feather. Feeling very pleased with himself, he looked around.

There were two strange lamps shining from the shadows under the tree. Plop went closer, and found that the lamps were a pair of unwinking eyes, and they belonged to a big black cat. Plop waited for a minute, but what he was expecting to happen didn't.

'Aren't you going to say anything?' he said at last. 'All the others did.'

'What should I say?' drawled the cat.

'Well, what did you think I was?' said Plop. 'I've been mistaken for a Catherine-wheel, and a thunderbolt, and a woolly ball, and a darling and a shooting star, and even a roly-poly pudding. Don't I remind you of anything?'

'You look like a baby owl to me,' said the cat. Then, seeing Plop's disappointed face, he added, 'but I *did* wonder for a moment whether it was starting to snow.'

'You thought I was a snowflake?' said Plop, brightening.

'Yes, but then when you landed, I saw that you looked more like a fat little snowman,' said the cat, 'and then I knew you were a baby owl.'

'Ah, but do you know what *kind* of owl I am?' said Plop.

'No,' admitted the cat, 'I can't say I do.'

'I am a barn owl,' Plop said.

'Really?' said the cat. 'Well, I'm a house cat, I suppose. My name is Orion.'

'Orion! The Great Hunter!' breathed Plop.

'Well, thank you,' said the cat, stroking his fine whiskers with a modest paw. 'I am rather a good mouser, as a matter of fact, but I didn't know I was as famous as that.'

'Orion,' said Plop again. 'Oh, I wish I had a name like that.'

'What is your name?' asked the cat.

'Plop,' said Plop. 'Isn't it awful?'

'Oh, I don't know – it's – er – different,' the cat said kindly, 'and at least it's short. There's nothing short for Orion really, so I'm usually called "Puss", which I can't say I care for.'

'I shall call you Orion,' said Plop.

'Thank you. Look – er – Plop. I was just going hunting. Would you like to come with me?'

'Oh,' said Plop. 'I don't know. I would like to, I think, but I'm not very happy about the dark.'

'Oh dear. We'll have to do something about that,' said Orion.

'What?' said Plop. 'What can you do when you're afraid of the dark?'

'I don't believe you are afraid of the dark, really,' said Orion. 'You just think you are. DARK IS BEAUTIFUL. Take a night like this. Look around you. Isn't it beautiful?'

Plop looked. The moon had risen. Everything was bathed in its white light.

'I love moonlight,' said the cat.

'Moonlight is magic. It turns everything it touches to silver, especially on frosty nights like this. Oh, come with me, Plop, and I will show you a beautiful world of sparkling silver – the secret night-time world of cats and owls. The daytime people are asleep. It is all ours, Plop. Will you come?'

'Yes!' said Plop. 'I will. Just wait while I tell Mummy where I'm going.' He flew like an arrow up to the landing branch.

'Well?' said his mother.

'Orion says that DARK IS BEAUTIFUL,

and he has asked me to go hunting with him. I can go, can't I, Mummy?'

'Of course, dear. But who is Orion?'

'The Great Hunter!' said Plop. 'See you later.'

When Mr Barn Owl came in from his first expedition, he found his wife a bit agitated.

'I think all that star-gazing has gone to Plop's head,' she said. 'He said he was going hunting with Orion the Great Hunter. That was one of the stars he showed us last night, wasn't it?'

'Well, I saw him just now with a perfectly ordinary black cat,' said Mr Barn Owl. 'They were pussy-footing it up among the chimney pots on those houses near the church.'

'So far from home – are you *sure* it was Plop you saw?' said Mrs Barn Owl.

It was indeed Plop he had seen. Orion had taken him up to his roof-top world, the cat leading the way, climbing and leaping, Plop fluttering behind.

They sat together on the highest roof and looked down over the sleeping town, a black velvet cat and a little white powder puff of owl.

'Well?' said the cat.

'It is – it is – oh, I haven't the words for it,' breathed Plop. 'But you are right, Orion. I am a night bird after all. Fancy sleeping all night and missing this!'

'And this is only one sort of night,' said Orion. 'There are lots of other kinds, all beautiful. There are hot, scented summer nights; and cold windy nights when the scuffling clouds make ragged shadows across the ground; and breathless, thundery nights which are suddenly slashed with jagged white lightning; and fresh spring nights, when even the day birds can't bear to sleep; and muffled winter nights when snow blankets the ground and ices the houses and trees. Oh, the nights I have seen – and you will see, Plop, as a night bird.'

'Yes,' said Plop. 'This is my world, Orion.

I must go home.'

'What, already? We haven't done any hunting yet, and I have lots more to show you – a glass lake with the moon floating in it, and . . .'

'I must go, Orion. I want to surprise them. Thank you for – for showing me that I'm a night bird.'

He bobbed his funny little bow and the black cat solemnly bowed back. 'Goodbye, Plop,' he said, 'and many, many Good Nights!'

Plop took off, circled once, gave a final 'Eek!' of farewell, and then flew, straight and sure, back to his tree.

'Well?' said his mother.

Plop took a deep breath. 'The small boy said DARK IS EXCITING. The old lady said DARK IS KIND. The Boy Scout said DARK IS FUN. The little girl said DARK IS NECESSARY. The Father Christmas Lady said DARK IS FASCINATING. The man with the telescope said DARK IS WONDERFUL and Orion the black cat says DARK IS BEAUTIFUL.'

'And what do you think, Plop?'

Plop looked up at his mother with

twinkling eyes. 'I think,' he said. 'I think – DARK IS SUPER! But sssh! Daddy's coming. Don't say anything.'

Mr Barn Owl came in with a great flapping of wings. He dropped something at Plop's feet.

Plop swallowed it in one gulp. 'That was nice,' he said. 'What was it?'

'A vole.'

'I like vole,' said Plop. 'What's next?'

'Why don't you come with me and find out?' said Mr Barn Owl.

'Yes, please,' said Plop.

Mr Barn Owl blinked. 'What did you say?'

'I said "yes, please",' Plop said. 'I would like to come hunting with you.'

'I thought you were afraid of the dark!'

'Me?' said Plop. 'Afraid of the dark!

That was a *long* time ago!'

'Well!' said his father. 'What are we waiting for? A-hunting we will go!'

'Hey, wait for me,' said Plop's mother. 'I'm coming too.'

So they took off together in the moonlight, Mr and Mrs Barn Owl on each side and Plop in the middle.

Plop – the night bird.

The Cat Who Wanted To Go Home

For Tricia and her children,

Joanna, Roderick and Caroline,

not forgetting D. H.

Contents

Le Bar
57

An unusual basket

Suzy was a little striped cat. She had stiffly starched white whiskers and a fine pair of football socks on her front paws.

Suzy lived in the house of a fisherman in a little seaside village in France. The fisherman had four sons. Pierre was ten years old, Henri was eight, Paul was six and Gaby was four, so when they stood in a row they looked like a set of steps. All the boys played with Suzy and they took her with them everywhere.

Pierre, the eldest one, made Suzy a scratching-post by wrapping a bit of old carpet round one of the fat legs of the big kitchen table. Suzy could sharpen her claws whenever she liked.

Henri knew which were the best tickly places on her spotted tummy. Although all the rest of her was covered with black stripes, Suzy's tummy was fawn with black spots. Henri said she was a tiger on top and a leopard underneath. Anyway, he was a jolly good tickler.

Paul made a toy for her. He tied a piece of crackly paper to the end of a long piece of string and pulled it along on the ground for her to chase. Suzy could run very fast and Paul could not keep ahead of her for very long. She would pounce and catch the paper again and again. Paul would stand still to get his breath back and dangle the bit of paper just out of reach above her head. Suzy would leap and leap to catch it, with Paul jerking it away when she got too near. Paul was great fun.

But Gaby, the youngest, was the best. Suzy adored him – and for a very odd reason. Gaby didn't know the proper way to stroke a cat. Most cats like being stroked from head to tail, the way the fur lies. But Gaby always stroked Suzy the wrong way – backwards from tail to head – and Suzy *loved* it. She would wriggle against his hand with delight, purring like a sewing machine, asking him to do it again and again. She liked it better than anything in the world. Yes, even better than eating fish. And Suzy liked eating fish very much indeed – which was just as well because she had it for breakfast and supper every day.

The boys always helped their father when he came home in his boat with his catch of fish. Every day they waited for him on the quay – Pierre and Henri and Paul and Gaby and Suzy.

She was allowed to eat as much as she wanted of the fish that were too small to be sold. There was always something for Suzy even when the catch wasn't very good. She would have grown fat if the boys had not given her so much exercise.

Suzy hated it when the boys were at school and there was nobody to play with her; nobody to dangle a bit of string or throw a ball or to climb trees with her. She would wander round the quay by herself getting in everybody's way, or go exploring in the fields behind the village.

One day she was chasing butterflies across a field when she nearly bumped into a huge basket. Suzy was used to baskets – there were lots of them on the quay – but this one was much bigger. Suzy climbed up the steep side and peered in. The basket was so big that there was a wooden stool inside. Under the stool was a nice patch of shade.

It was a very hot day. Suzy decided to have a little nap. She jumped lightly down into the basket and settled herself nose to tail under the stool. Curled round like that she looked like a huge furry snail.

Suzy was soon fast asleep.

When she woke up Suzy felt very peculiar. The basket seemed to be rocking from side to side, joggling her. She rushed to the edge of the basket and climbed up the side to jump out – but she changed her mind when she looked over the top! The ground was a very long way away – much too far for her to jump. She clung on tightly as the basket jerked again, grabbing at a rope with her paws.

Ropes? She had not noticed them when she climbed in. Suzy looked up. The ropes were attached to a huge balloon – an *enormous* balloon. Suzy was floating high up in the sky in a basket suspended from a balloon!

Poor Suzy! She slid back into the basket and crouched on the floor, shivering with fright.

Then she felt a gentle hand on her back and looked up to find that there was a man in the basket with her.

'Hello, little cat,' he said. 'I didn't invite you! Oh well, it's too late now. You will have to come with me to England.'

Suzy didn't know where England was, but she knew she didn't want to go there. She wanted to stay in France in her own little fishing village with the boys.

'Chez-moi!' she wailed. It sounded like 'shay-mwa'. She was saying in French that she wanted to go home.

But the man had to jump up to do something with the balloon, which was swinging wildly, and from then on was too busy to take any notice of his little passenger.

So Suzy floated across the sea between France and England by balloon! She hated every joggly moment of it. The worst part was seeing the coast of France disappear behind them – France and Pierre and Henri and Paul and Gaby, France and everything she knew and loved.

'Chez-moi!' she wailed again, but nobody heard her. There were big puffy clouds sailing underneath them and sometimes what looked like toy ships on the sea far below. It was really very interesting and beautiful, but Suzy could only think about one thing. How was she going to get back across this huge stretch of water?

They landed in England with a bump. Suzy had not realised that they were back over land again because for the last bit she had had her eyes tightly shut. She jumped out of the basket and ran. She could not get away from that balloon fast enough.

Because she was very hungry, she ran towards a fishy smell. But the smell was coming from the sea and there were no fish and no fishing boats. This was an English seaside town and not a bit like her own village. There was just a wide expanse of concrete in front of the sea, with steps down to the sand. Poor Suzy. She sat miserably on the sea-front looking out at the waves. How was she going to get home across all that water?

Luckily an RSPCA lady came along. It was her job to find homes for lost cats. She picked up Suzy and took her to the house of a kind old lady whom she knew, called Auntie Jo. 'Do you think you could look after this little cat for me, Auntie Jo?' the RSPCA lady said. 'I've never seen her before. She's not from around here. She must be lost.'

'Of course she can stay with me,' said Auntie Jo. 'She'll be company for Biff.'

Biff was Auntie Jo's new budgie who was just learning to talk.

'Hello, Auntie Jo,' he said in his funny cracked voice.

Of course, Suzy could not understand English, but she understood the saucer of milk that Auntie Jo put down for her and she lapped up every drop. Then, because she was a polite cat, she said 'thank you' in French: 'Merci!' It was a miaowing sound, 'mare-see'.

'What a funny miaow you have, Pussy cat,' said Auntie Jo.

'Merci,' said Biff.

'Oh, clever Biff,' Auntie Jo said.

'Clever Biff,' said Biff. 'Merci.'

Suzy was made very comfortable on an

old chair that night. Auntie Jo stroked her gently and Suzy purred. She purred in French, but purring sounds the same all over the world, whatever country you come from.

But it wasn't like home. She did miss Gaby stroking her the wrong way.

Up and down is no good

So Suzy came to live with Auntie Jo and Biff.

Next morning Auntie Jo got out her tricycle to go shopping. It was a great big one with huge wheels and a basket on the front. Auntie Jo felt that she was too old to wobble about on a bicycle any more, and what was good enough for the little girl next door was good enough for her.

When Suzy saw Auntie Jo standing in

front of the mirror in the hall, fiercely jabbing a hat pin into her flat straw hat to keep it anchored to her bun, she guessed that Auntie Jo was going out.

When Auntie Jo had pedalled a few yards down the road she suddenly saw a whiskery face staring at her over the handlebars.

'Chez-moi!' it said.

Auntie Jo swerved violently and stopped.

'Oh, Pussy! You did frighten me. What are you doing in there? Go home. Shoo!'

Suzy didn't understand.

'Chez-moi!' she wailed again, settling herself more comfortably in the basket.

'Oh, very well, you can come if you want to,' said Auntie Jo, starting to pedal again. 'But sit still.'

So Suzy rode down to the sea-front in

great style in Auntie Jo's tricycle basket. She got very excited when she saw the sea. That sheet of blue water with white lace trimmings was all that lay between her and France. Oh, she would soon be home.

The minute Auntie Jo had parked the tricycle by the butcher's shop and disappeared inside, Suzy jumped down from the basket and ran across the road to the beach. There were children everywhere, digging in the sand and running about with buckets of water, just like French children. Suzy dodged nimbly between them and ran down to the water's edge. She had hoped to find a fishing boat like the one belonging to her family, but there didn't seem to be anything like that – only lots of people shouting and splashing in the water. She was so busy staring out to sea, looking for boats, that she hardly noticed the wavelets trickling across the sand and washing over her paws.

'Oh, look! There's a kitten over there, paddling!' a little girl said to her father, who was sitting in a deckchair reading his paper.

'Kittens don't paddle, Caroline,' he said. 'Cats hate water.'

'Well, this one is paddling,' said Caroline. 'I'm going down to watch her.'

She dropped her spade and ran down to the sea. Suzy had moved along a bit, but she was easy to find because of the trail of paw-prints she left behind her in the sand.

'Pussy!' said Caroline, putting down her hand and stroking Suzy. Suzy trilled and purred and rubbed against the little girl's hand.

'Oh, you are sweet,' she said, picking her up and holding her against her shoulder. 'Come on, I want to show you to Daddy. He doesn't believe that you've been paddling.'

She started back up the beach, but Suzy suddenly jumped down and tore away across the sand towards some rocks. She had seen something! From Caroline's shoulder she had had a better view over the top of people's heads, and she was sure she had seen a boat. A boat! She could get home at last.

Caroline started to follow her, but Suzy was going much too fast, and anyway her father would be cross if she just disappeared without telling him where she was going. Bother! Now he would never believe that there *had* been a paddling kitten.

Suzy reached the rocks, and looked about

her. Yes! There was the boat. It was a very small plastic canoe, but it was all there was so it would have to do. A small boy was paddling it along close to the rocks. Suzy scrambled towards him over the slippery seaweed and fixed him with her great green eyes.

'Chez-moi!' she called hopefully. 'Chez-moi!'

The boy looked up and stared at her in amazement. He had never seen a cat on the beach before.

'What do you want, Puss? Not a ride, surely?'

Suzy answered by taking a firm grip on the seaweed and leaping neatly into the canoe. She curled her tail round her toes and waited patiently. She was on her way home at last.

But of course she was not. People don't

cross the Channel in toy canoes. The little boy was only allowed to go up and down in the shallow water close to the shore. After a few minutes of going up and down, up and down, Suzy began to get restless. This was no good. This wouldn't get her home to France.

'Chez-moi!' she wailed. Why didn't the boy understand how important it was to her to get home? 'Chez-moi!'

'Oh, you want to get out now, do you?' he said. 'Right'o, hang on a tick.'

He pulled in towards a flat rock. When Suzy realised that he was taking her back to land she gave up all hope of getting to France on this trip. She got ready to spring.

'Mind your claws!' shouted the little boy suddenly, as he saw her digging them into the plastic canoe. 'You'll puncture us!'

It was too late, and Suzy didn't understand anyway. She sprang out on to the rock, leaving behind four sets of tiny holes from which the air hissed fiercely. Claws are not good for inflated plastic.

The boy sprang out too, pulling the canoe after him.

'That's the last time I give a ride to a cat,' he grumbled, fishing in his pocket for his repair kit.

The canoe slowly collapsed and was quite flat by the time Suzy was back by the butcher's shop. Auntie Jo's tricycle wasn't there, but Suzy remembered the way to her house.

'Pussy cat, Pussy cat, where have you been?' said Auntie Jo when Suzy walked in.

'Pussy cat, Pussy cat, where have you been?' Biff repeated in his funny voice. 'Clever Biff.'

'You are a clever Biff,' said Auntie Jo. 'Well, Pussy cat, here is your dinner.' She put down a saucer of liver.

Suzy ate it all up. It wasn't fish, but it was very nice.

'Merci,' she said, cleaning her whiskers.

'You do have a funny miaow,' said Auntie Jo.

'Merci,' Biff said. 'Clever Biff.'

And Suzy purred.

But she did miss Gaby stroking her the wrong way.

They do it for fun

Next morning Auntie Jo got out her tricycle again. Suzy hopped into the basket. It was very windy and Auntie Jo had to hang on to her hat all the way down to the shops.

As they came round the corner on to the sea-front they were nearly knocked over. The wind was blowing fiercely from the sea. There were huge waves thundering on the beach.

Auntie Jo managed to park by the

grocer's. Suzy went to look at the waves. There would be no chance of getting home to France that day.

Or was there? A young man was pushing his way into the waves holding a flat board above his head. He was definitely going out to sea *towards France*!

Suzy ran towards him, but she was too late; he was already a long way out. He was swimming now, pushing the board in front of him.

She watched him sadly. He was going without her. She had so wanted to go home. Suzy threw back her head and wailed:

'Chez-moi!'

But what was this? The young man must have heard her, because he was coming back. He was coming back for her!

Suzy ran to meet him, not caring how wet she got. He jumped off the board as it grounded on the sand, and Suzy jumped on to it. The young man *was* surprised.

'Do you want to come surfing with me?' he asked. 'I thought cats didn't like water!'

'Chez-moi!' Suzy said.

'OK. Hang on, though. It's kind of wet out there.'

The young man lifted the surfboard with Suzy on it high above his head, and set off through the waves.

Suzy had to work hard at keeping her balance, but she was happy. France at last.

She was not quite so happy when the young man began swimming, pushing the board in front of him, sometimes *through* the waves. But Suzy just closed her eyes and hung on, spitting out the nasty sea water when she got a mouthful.

Suddenly the young man shouted, 'Here comes a beauty!'

He swung the board round, kneeled on it, and then stood up. A huge wave picked them up and hurtled them back toward the beach – to England. Suzy was furious.

'Chez-moi!' she wailed.

'Yes, isn't it marvellous!' shouted the young man. He thought she was enjoying it as much as he was.

There were some more young men with boards on the beach. They were very surprised to see Suzy.

'Whatever have you got there, Bill?' shouted one of them. 'A new member for the club?'

'Yes,' Bill shouted. 'She's terrific. A real swinger. You watch.'

They all set off out to sea. Suzy was very relieved. Of course, he had just come back for the others, that was all. Now they would go to France.

But, of course, they didn't. They went out to sea and back again several times before Suzy realised that they were only doing it for fun!

The surf-riders thought Suzy was wonderful, and when they came out of the sea for lunch they made a great fuss of her. They rolled her in a towel to dry her off a bit and then fed her with a whole tin of sardines. Fish! Then they played ball with her and pulled a belt along the sand for her to chase.

Suzy had a lovely time – even if she didn't get home to France.

When she walked into Auntie Jo's house, Biff said:

'Pussy cat, Pussy cat, where have you been?'

'Yes, where have you been?' said Auntie Jo. 'Swimming, by the look of you. There's seaweed on your tail.'

Suzy sat down and washed herself all over. Auntie Jo pulled off the seaweed. Then she put down a saucer of mince.

Suzy ate it all up. It wasn't fish, but it was very good.

'Merci,' she said, cleaning her whiskers.

'You do have a funny miaow,' Auntie Jo said.

And Suzy purred.

But she did miss Gaby stroking her the wrong way.

Catty paddle

The next morning Auntie Jo got out her tricycle and Suzy hopped into the basket.

'I'm not sure that I should take you with me,' said Auntie Jo. 'You came back in such a horrible mess yesterday.'

'Chez-moi!' Suzy said, wondering why Auntie Jo didn't start.

'Oh, all right,' said Auntie Jo, 'but you behave yourself today.'

She pedalled off towards the shops. The wind had dropped, and when they came round the corner to the sea-front the sea was flat and calm like glass. Suzy was out of the basket before Auntie Jo had finished parking.

'Oh dear, she's off again,' said Auntie Jo, watching Suzy run down towards the sea. 'She is a funny little cat.'

The funny little cat was looking for *boats*. There must be some boats going to France on a nice calm day like this.

There were some pedal boats going up and down, but Suzy was getting wise. She knew that up and down was no good to her. She needed a boat that was going out to sea.

And there was one – a very fast speedboat. It was pulling a young girl along behind it! She was riding on the water on two long thin boards. She was going very fast. A boat like that would get you to France in no time.

Suzy ran down to the end of the pier. There was another speedboat getting ready to go, and there was another girl getting ready to be pulled behind.

Suzy watched her. She had hoped that one of the boats would pull *her* behind it, but those long water-skis were much too big for her.

Then the girl got hold of a piece of rope that was dangling from the back of the speedboat. Suzy wouldn't be able to hang on to that either, not with her tiny paws.

There was only one thing for it – she would have to go along with the girl.

Suzy jumped. She landed on the girl's shoulder, very gently, but the girl was not at all pleased.

'Get off!' she cried. 'What on earth . . .?' She looked down sideways at her shoulder to see what this furry thing was, but she dare not let go of the rope to push it off because they would be starting any second.

'Oh get off!' she said again, trying to shove Suzy with her chin, but Suzy was not going to be pushed off that easily.

Then it was too late. With a great roar, the speedboat burst away from the pier. The girl tightened her grip on the rope and struggled to keep her balance on the skis, with Suzy teetering on her shoulder.

There were lots of people on the pier watching the water-skiers, and they all laughed when they saw Suzy.

'A water-skiing cat!' they said. 'Just look at that!'

The water-skiing cat was having great difficulty in staying on. What could she hang on to? The girl had long hair. Suzy managed to get one paw tangled up in it and hung on to that.

'Ow!' cried the poor girl, but there was nothing she could do about it.

Suzy began to enjoy herself. It was very exciting going so fast, and she wasn't really getting wet at all except for a little spray. Oh, this was a lovely way to go home to France.

Then she noticed something. The other boat had turned round and was going back to the pier! Were they going to do the same?

Yes, their speedboat began to swerve. Suzy was so disappointed.

'Chez-moi!' she wailed loudly into the girl's ear.

It was too much for her. She jumped, lost her balance, and a second later she and Suzy were struggling in the water, the speedboat heading back for the pier without them.

Suzy headed for the pier too. She discovered that she could swim! She did a catty sort of dog-paddle.

Meanwhile, the crew in the boat realised that they had lost the water-skier and came back to pick her up.

'What happened to you?' asked the driver as he helped her into the boat.

'It was that wretched cat!' she said. 'It was all its fault.'

'What cat?' said the man. 'I can't see any cat.'

'Oh dear, she must have drowned, the poor little thing!' The water-skier was suddenly contrite. 'I was so busy trying to keep afloat myself I didn't notice what happened to her.'

'I did,' said the other man in the boat.

'She's swimming. Look! She's nearly at the pier already.'

There was Suzy, sodden and dripping, climbing on to the pier. All the people were cheering. The water-skier was so relieved that Suzy wasn't drowned that she forgave her at once.

Suzy dodged all the people and ran home to Auntie Jo.

'Pussy cat, Pussy cat, where have you been?' said Biff.

'You might well ask!' Auntie Jo said. She looked in horror at the soggy Suzy, dripping on her carpet. 'She's in an even worse state than she was yesterday.'

She rubbed Suzy all over hard with a rough towel and put on an electric fire for her to sit by until she was really dry.

Then she gave Suzy her dinner – a saucer of rabbit.

'I'm not sure you deserve it, though,' Auntie Jo said.

Suzy ate it all up. It wasn't fish, but it was very good.

'Merci,' she said, cleaning her whiskers.

Then Auntie Jo gave her a saucer of milk. It was lovely after all that salty water.

'Merci,' she said again.

'You do have a funny miaow,' Auntie Jo said. 'But you're a funny cat altogether.' She stroked her and Suzy purred.

But she did miss Gaby stroking her the wrong way.

The wettest way

The next morning Auntie Jo opened her newspaper – and there was a photograph of Suzy water-skiing!

'Well! So that's what you were up to yesterday, Pussy cat!' she said. 'No wonder you were so wet. I think you had better stay at home today.'

But when Auntie Jo wheeled out her tricycle, Suzy popped into the basket as usual.

'Chez-moi!' she said to Auntie Jo, beseeching her with her big green eyes.

'Oh, come on then,' Auntie Jo said.

As they pedalled along the sea-front to the shops, a lady and her husband recognised Suzy.

'Why surely that's the little cat who was water-skiing yesterday,' they said. 'So she belongs to you, does she, Auntie Jo?'

'She's a stray,' Auntie Jo said. 'I'm just feeding her.'

'Well, she's a very good swimmer,' said the lady.

'Yes,' said her husband. 'Let's hope she doesn't get any ideas because of what's happening today.'

'What is happening?' asked Auntie Jo.

'There's a swimmer attempting to cross

the Channel. That's a very long way for a small cat.'

'Did you hear that, Pussy cat?' said Auntie Jo. 'No Channel swimming.'

But I'm afraid Suzy didn't understand, and when Auntie Jo parked her tricycle, she popped out of the basket as usual and ran down to the water's edge.

She was looking for boats, of course. There was one small boat and beside it was a great big fat man. It was the Channel swimmer. Somebody was smearing him all over with greasy stuff to keep him warm during his long swim.

Suzy wasn't very interested in all this until she heard somebody say, 'Well, good luck, Jim! Let's hope you get to France.'

France? He was really going to France!

So it was hardly surprising that when the man had been swimming for a few minutes he found that there was a little cat swimming beside him!

The man was swimming very slowly and steadily because he had a long way to go, but even so it was a bit fast for Suzy, who was having to paddle madly to keep up with him.

Clearly she wouldn't be able to do this for very long.

'Go home!' grunted the man.

Suzy didn't understand him, and anyway going home was what she was doing!

'What did you say, Jim?' said his wife, who was going along in the boat to see that he was all right.

'Company,' said Jim. 'Look!'

His wife thought he meant sharks or something.

'Good heavens!' she said. 'Where?'

'Cat,' said Jim.

'Cat?' Jim's wife peered through the waves. Then she saw Suzy.

Suzy was holding her head as high as she could with her ears folded down to keep out the water. Jim's wife did laugh.

'You look like a mother duck and its baby, Jim,' she said. 'Shall I pick her up?'

'Leave her,' said Jim. 'She's doing fine. I like having her.'

And so Suzy swam the Channel for a bit.

But she began to get very tired and she was afraid of being left behind. The man kept having to wait for her to catch up.

'Maisie, pick her up,' Jim said at last. 'She's slowing me down.'

Suzy felt herself being scooped up out of the water.

'Chez-moi!' she wailed furiously. She ran to the edge of the boat, dived in and started swimming again.

Jim nearly choked. It is very difficult to laugh when you are swimming. Maisie scooped up Suzy once again and this time she trapped her under a lobster pot at the bottom of the boat.

'She seems to be as silly about wanting to swim the Channel as you are!' Maisie said.

Suzy didn't like the lobster pot, but she was so exhausted that she hadn't the energy to fight it for long. She lay down and sulked.

'That's better,' Maisie said. 'You're much too small to swim such a long way. You stay here with me.' She took her out and dried her and wrapped her in a warm towel, keeping a firm hold on her.

It dawned on Suzy at last that the boat was following the swimmer. So she *was* going to France, and really it was much easier to go there on Maisie's lap than by swimming. She settled down happily.

Maisie looked at her watch. 'You're making good time, Jim,' she called out. 'We should catch the tide.'

But she spoke too soon. The wind started to get up and the sea got rougher and rougher. Jim found it more and more difficult to move forward. In the end it got so bad that he was hardly moving at all, and Maisie had to turn off the boat's engine to stay with him. The boat began to be tossed about, too, as the waves got bigger and bigger, and Maisie put Suzy back under the lobster pot to keep her safe.

Jim struggled on for a bit, but it was no good. He would have missed the tide now anyway.

Suzy couldn't believe it when she saw

him being helped into the boat, and when the boat turned round and headed back for England it was the last straw.

'Chez-moi!' she cried, heartbroken. 'Chez-moi!

'I'm sorry, Pussy,' said Jim. 'I thought you were going to bring me luck, but it seems that I was wrong. Never mind. I'll try again tomorrow.'

Suzy only knew that she wasn't going home to France.

'Chez-moi!'

'There, she's telling me she's sorry,' said Jim. He put on a thick sweater and some trousers and had a cup of coffee. Now that the engine was full on, the boat wasn't tossing nearly so much, so Jim took Suzy out of the lobster pot and she rode the rest of the way back to England on his lap. He made a great fuss of her.

'She had plenty of guts, this little one,' he said to Maisie. 'Maybe she couldn't swim the Channel, but I bet she could swim the Thames. I can see it now in *The Guinness Book of Records*: "First cat to swim the Thames in the record-breaking time of five minutes". What about that, Pussy cat?' He stroked Suzy's ears. Suzy purred and then fell fast asleep.

When she woke up they were back at the pier.

'Hard luck, Jim,' people were saying. 'Are you going to try again?'

'Tomorrow if the weather's kind,' he said. 'I think I'll take my lucky cat with me.' He looked around. 'Oh, where is she?'

Suzy had slipped away in the crowd and

run home to Auntie Jo.

'Pussy cat, Pussy cat, where have you been?' said Biff.

'Swimming the Channel by the look of her!' Auntie Jo said. 'Oh, Pussy cat, you are a shocker.'

'Shocker!' said Biff. 'Shocker! Clever Biff.'

Auntie Jo dried Suzy again and gave her her dinner – a piece of chicken. Suzy ate it all up. It wasn't fish, but it was very good.

'Merci,' she said, cleaning her whiskers.

'Merci,' said Biff, 'shocker!'

And Suzy purred.

But she did miss Gaby stroking her the wrong way.

Suzy nearly goes under

The next morning Suzy waited patiently in the hall by the door while Auntie Jo speared her hat to her bun. It was a different hat today – a flowery one. Auntie Jo saw Suzy reflected in the glass.

'Now, Pussy cat,' she said. 'It's no good you waiting there today. It's Sunday – I'm going to church. I'm not taking you with me.'

But of course, she was. Suzy settled

herself into the basket the minute Auntie Jo had wheeled out her tricycle, and nothing Auntie Jo said or did would move her.

'All right,' said Auntie Jo at last. 'Come – but you'll have to wait outside during the service.'

'Chez-moi!' replied Suzy, quite happy.

Auntie Jo went a different way today, turning out of the town. The church was at the top of a hill and Auntie Jo had to get off and push the tricycle for the last bit. Suzy didn't mind. She sat up in the basket and looked about her. The church was on a headland – a piece of land which stuck out into the sea – and Suzy could see into the bay on the other side. There were ships there, big ships!

The moment Auntie Jo parked the tricycle by the church porch Suzy was off like a rocket over the headland.

'Oh dear,' said Auntie Jo. 'I hope she doesn't go down to the sea again.'

Suzy took a short cut down a cliff path, streaked across the sand and up some steps to a big quay. There was a smart motor-boat decorated with flags just about to leave the jetty. Suzy jumped neatly down and settled herself behind a pile of rope.

With a roar the motor-boat shot off across the bay, a plume of white foam behind it. There were a lot of men in uniform on board, including an Admiral, but of course Suzy didn't notice that. All she knew was that they were going towards France!

Or were they? The boat was drawing up alongside a very odd sausage-shaped ship. Oh well, perhaps she'd still get there.

Suzy joined the end of the procession that was going aboard the ship. The sailors already on the ship were all lined up ready to be inspected by the Admiral. Someone was making an awful piping noise on a funny kind of whistle.

The Admiral began to strut importantly between the lines of men. Suzy, who was determined not to be left behind, trotted importantly behind him, for all the world as if inspecting the fleet was something she did every day of her life. Eyes front, tail erect, her football-sock paws lifting neatly as she stepped along the deck, Suzy was almost as dignified as the Admiral himself – and he had all his gold braid to help him!

The men were trying hard not to grin; it was not often that they had to stand to attention to be inspected by a small tabby cat!

By the end of the inspection Suzy was beginning to feel a little impatient. What was all this walking about for? Why didn't they get on with it and make for France?

Well, they did begin to get on with something. The Admiral went back to his motor-boat to be taken ashore. Suzy didn't want *that* so she ran and hid behind a sort of tower.

When the Admiral's boat had gone, the ship's Captain gave the order: 'Make ready to submerge!' Of course, Suzy didn't know what that meant.

The sailors rushed about slamming doors and hatches. Suddenly Suzy was the only one left on top of the ship. The men had all disappeared.

Well, as long as she got to France, Suzy didn't mind having a lonely ride.

But what was happening? The ship was sinking! Suzy watched with horror as the ship went down, down and the water came up, up towards her. Soon the main part of the ship had completely disappeared and although Suzy had scrambled to the top of the tower thing, that was sinking too!

Poor Suzy. She clung to the last bit sticking out of the top and stared at the empty sea around her. The shore was terribly far away.

Inside the submarine the Captain took a last look through the periscope.

'Funny!' he said. 'I can't see a thing. There seems to be something blocking it.'

'Let's have a look,' said the First Officer. 'Good heavens! The Admiral's moggy! We'll have to surface'.

'Moggy?' the Captain said. 'What is a . . .?'

'Cat,' said the First Officer. 'You remember; the one that inspected us. I thought he would have taken her ashore with him. Careless chap. Oh well. Surface?'

'Yes,' sighed the Captain. 'Someone will have to take her ashore.'

So Suzy found herself slowly rising as the ship came to the top of the water again.

It *was* a relief! But what were they up to? It really was a most peculiar ship, sinking and un-sinking itself like this. Suzy didn't like it at all.

So she wasn't too upset when a sailor picked her off the conning-tower and took her into a rubber dinghy. It had an outboard motor and they were soon back at the quay. Suzy had leapt out and was nearly halfway back to Auntie Jo's house before the sailor had had time to secure the dinghy to the harbour wall.

'I was afraid you were lost at sea,' said Auntie Jo when Suzy walked in. 'I nearly cried in church when we sang a hymn about "those in peril on the sea".' She sang the last bit in a quavery voice. Biff sang it after her in an even more quavery voice.

'For those in peril on the sea. Clever Biff'.

'Oh you are a clever Biff,' said Auntie Jo. 'On the sea. On the sea. Clever Biff. On the sea.' Biff liked singing.

Auntie Jo put a saucer down for Suzy, who had nearly been in peril *under* the sea. It was chicken giblets. It wasn't fish, but it was very good. Suzy ate it all up.

'Merci,' she said, cleaning her whiskers.

'You have got a funny miaow,' Auntie Jo said.

'Merci,' said Biff, and then he began to sing. 'On the sea. On the sea. Clever Biff. On the sea.'

Auntie Jo and Suzy were just a little tired of that hymn by bedtime.

Before she went upstairs, Auntie Jo stroked Suzy 'good night'.

Suzy purred.

But she did miss Gaby stroking her the wrong way.

Home by car?

The next morning Auntie Jo got out her tricycle as usual. Suzy popped into the basket, but then jumped out again and went back into the house. She felt that she ought to say goodbye to Biff because she was *sure* that she would get home to France today.

'Au revoir,' she said, which is French for 'goodbye'.

Biff cocked his head to one side.

'Clever Biff!' said Biff. 'Hello, Auntie Jo.'

Suzy felt that he hadn't got it quite right. When you say goodbye to somebody they usually say goodbye back to you. So she tried again.

'Au revoir.'

This time Biff got it. 'Au revoir!' he said. 'Clever Biff. Au revoir.'

Suzy ran out and was only just in time to catch Auntie Jo, who was already out of the gate.

'I thought you had decided not to come today,' Auntie Jo said as she stopped for Suzy to hop in.

'Chez-moi,' said Suzy.

'You have got a funny miaow,' Auntie Jo said.

They pedalled off down to the shops on

the sea-front. Auntie Jo parked the tricycle outside the baker's shop. As she got down from the saddle she turned to Suzy who was poised to jump out of the basket.

'I wonder where you are off to this time?' she said. 'Well, I suppose we will see you at supper,' and she went into the baker's shop.

Suzy jumped down and hurried across the road. She had just spotted something familiar on the other side. It was a French sailor with a bobble on his cap! A French sailor might lead her to a French ship. Suzy began to follow him along the pavement.

The sailor was walking very fast; Suzy had to keep running to keep up with him. They seemed to be going a very long way. After a while the pavement became more crowded and the traffic going past them got heavier and noisier. Suzy realised that they were coming to a big port. She could see cranes and wharves and the masts and funnels of ships.

Ships! Suzy kept as close to her sailor as she could. Oh, surely he would lead her to a French ship!

Poor Suzy. He didn't lead her to a French ship. She lost him altogether for he turned into a large building and disappeared. Suzy tried to follow him, but there was a swing door, and when she tried to go through, it just swung her right round and back on to the step again! She tried again and the same thing happened.

Oh, well. She didn't need the sailor now. He had led her to a port. One of those ships *must* be going to France.

Suzy trotted along a wide road towards the quays where the ships were. There were lots of cars going the same way. One of them drew up at the kerb near Suzy and the driver called out to a man in uniform.

'Is this the way for the ferry to France?'

'That's right, sir. Just keep straight ahead,' said the man.

France! Suzy must stay with this car. As the car moved off again she began to run. It was much harder than following the sailor – Suzy ran and ran until her paws ached.

She was almost giving up when the car slowed to a halt. There was a queue of cars waiting to board the ferry. Suzy had not expected to go home to France by car, but it looked as if that was what she was going to have to do. She ran along the queue looking for a car that she could get inside without being noticed.

She found the very one. The family it belonged to had brought so much luggage that the boot would not shut properly and was tied half-open with rope. This left room for Suzy to nose her way in between a suitcase and a deckchair and find a nice little space where she could curl up. The family in the car behind might have noticed her, but luckily they were busy looking at a map of France to see where they would have to go when they got to the other side of the Channel.

Suzy's car moved slowly forwards. Suddenly there was a great clanking as they went down the ramp and into the hold of the ship. It was dark down there, but there were some lights on. Suzy kept very still, a bit frightened by all the banging and clanging as people got out and slammed their car doors. There were cars behind and cars in front and cars on each side. The slams echoed round the metal sides of the ship.

Suzy's family got out of the car and disappeared through a little door in the side where everybody else was going.

At last it was quiet. Suzy peeped out. There was nobody about. She squeezed between a couple of cars and made for the door that her family had gone through.

But there was a new noise. Suzy stopped and listened. It was the ship's engines. They were off!

Suzy hurried on up some steep stairs and came out into a corridor. This led into a big room full of people sitting at tables and eating. Suzy thought it was a very funny ship – more like a house. Then she saw some more stairs. Could there be bedrooms up there? Suzy climbed up and came out on deck into the sunlight.

There was sea all around them. Suzy ran to the rail that went round the side of the ship and then along it to the stern at the back. She could see England disappearing behind them!

She ran down the other side to the very front of the ship, the bows, and found herself a piece of curled-up rope to sit on.

Suzy sat there, her eyes set towards France. She was going home at last.

Home at last

There was Suzy, sitting like a figurehead in the bows of the ship, getting nearer to France every minute.

A little girl came and sat with her. 'Are you the ship's cat?' she asked.

'Chez-moi!' said Suzy.

'You do have a funny miaow,' said the little girl. 'Granny, look. I've found the ship's cat, and she's got such a funny miaow. You listen.'

Suzy didn't say anything else. She had explained where she was going.

'Perhaps she'd like a bit of sardine sandwich,' Granny said.

Suzy did like it. She ate it all up and cleaned her whiskers.

'Merci,' she said.

'I told you she'd got a funny miaow,' the little girl said to her granny.

Lots of other children came and talked to Suzy, but she didn't move from her position in the bows, which was the nearest she could get to France.

It seemed a very long time, but at last a thin line of land appeared ahead of them.

'Look! Look! There's France!' the little girl shouted, pointing.

France! Suzy could hardly believe it.

Soon she would be home.

Just then a sailor came along – and he saw Suzy.

'What's that cat doing there?' he said.

'It's the ship's cat,' said the little girl. 'Didn't you know?'

'No, I didn't,' the sailor said. 'We haven't got a ship's cat. She's a stowaway.'

He reached forward and made a grab at Suzy. Suzy dodged him. He didn't look friendly at all. He wasn't.

He chased her all around the ship – down the stairs, along corridors, through the dining-room, past the shop and back up on deck again.

Soon all the children began to join in. They thought it was a wonderful game.

Poor Suzy. She was so near home. Nothing must stop her now. She must hide, but where? Anyway, the mob of laughing, shouting children was too close behind her.

Then she saw the mast. She ran up it like a squirrel and clung at the very top. Everyone stopped and looked up. No one could reach her.

'I'll get her down,' said the puffing sailor. He went off to fetch a ladder.

Suzy stared around her desperately. There was France getting nearer and nearer – France and home.

Then she saw something else. In the sea ahead of them was a French fishing boat.

And on the deck were four little boys like steps.

It was Suzy's family! It must be.

'Out of the way there!' said the sailor, clearing the children from the foot of the mast. He had come back with a ladder.

But Suzy didn't notice. She leapt straight over his head on to the deck, ran to the rail – and dived!

'Oooooh!' said everybody watching.

'She'll drown!' cried the little girl. 'Somebody save her! Quick!'

But Suzy didn't drown. She seemed to go a very, very long way down into the green water, and then she paddled hard with her little paws and came up to the surface like a cork.

She began to swim. The ship's side towered above her, with a row of faces along the rail. Suzy couldn't see the fishing boat any more because of the waves, but she swam towards the place where she had seen it last.

The little girl waved her arms madly at the boys on the fishing boat and pointed down to Suzy.

'Cat overboard!' she shouted.

The other children joined her: 'Cat overboard!'

The little French boys did not understand, but they saw that the children were pointing to something in the sea. They got their father to turn towards it.

At last there was a calm stretch of water between two waves and the boys spotted something moving there. In a few seconds Suzy was scooped out of the sea with a bucket.

The ferry was already some way away, but they could hear the children cheering because Suzy was safe, and see them waving goodbye.

Suzy was more than safe – she was very, very happy. She sat there in the bucket purring like a ship's engine.

'It's a cat!' said Pierre. 'A swimming cat!'

'Stripey,' said Henri.

'With football socks,' said Paul.

'It's Suzy!' said Gaby, lifting her tenderly out of the bucket and holding her close. 'I knew she would come back.'

That evening, in England, Auntie Jo was getting worried. No Suzy.

'I wonder where she is?' she said aloud. 'She's never missed her dinner before.'

'Shocker!' said Biff. 'Hello, Auntie Jo.

Au revoir!'

'What did you say?' Auntie Jo said.

'Clever Biff. Au revoir. Au revoir.'

'Now where did you learn that?' said Auntie Jo. 'I've not taught you that. Of course, she did have a funny miaow. I wonder . . .'

And the French cat that Auntie Jo was wondering about? She was so full of fish that she could hardly move. She was on the rug in the boys' bedroom in France, being watched by four pairs of shining eyes. She was purring and purring as though she would never stop. Gaby was stroking her the wrong way!

Suzy was home at last.

The Hen Who Wouldn't Give Up

For Dr Frederick N. Hicks who, like Hilda,

never gives up, and D.H. likewise

Contents

Hilda has an upsetting morning

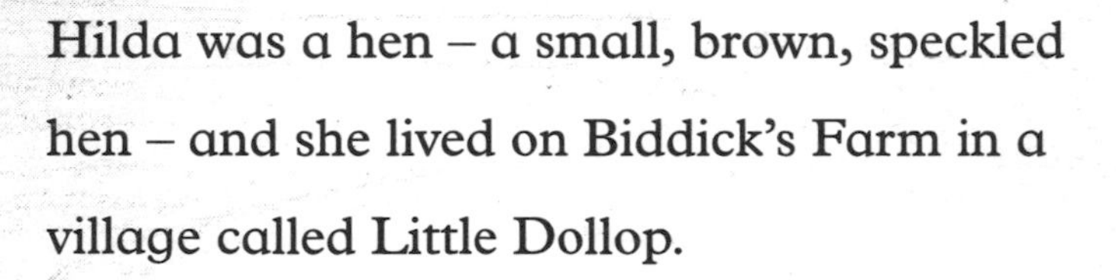

Hilda was a hen – a small, brown, speckled hen – and she lived on Biddick's Farm in a village called Little Dollop.

Hilda was very excited. Her auntie had just hatched out five baby chicks. Hilda was dying to see them. The trouble was, her auntie lived in Much Wallop, and that was five miles away. How was Hilda going to get there? It was too far to walk.

She sat in her favourite spot under the hedge and had a good think.

Suddenly Hilda perked up her head. Of course! She would have to get a lift.

She squeezed through the hedge and hurried down the muddy lane from the farm.

There'll be lots of cars and things on the main road, she said to herself. I'll be in Much Wallop in no time. Won't Auntie be surprised to see me!

But when Hilda reached the road there was nothing in sight.

Perhaps I shall find something further on,

she thought, and set off in the direction of Much Wallop.

She was in luck. Just around the corner there was a row of cottages, and parked in front of them was a big, green, lorry thing.

It was rather an odd box-like shape, with an open half-door at the back. Hilda hopped on to this and peered inside. She could not see very clearly, but it seemed to be full of torn packets and ashes and old tins. It smelled very nasty.

Still, this was no time to be fussy. Hilda hopped daintily down and settled on an old cornflake packet.

There were a few cornflakes left in it. Hilda was very fond of cornflakes.

She was just finishing the last one when she had a terrible shock. There was a great clanging and banging, and then a shower of horrible things was poured on top of her! She was battered and bumped by rotten apples and sticky baked-bean tins and spiky fish-bones and – ugh! – all sorts of unspeakable things. Hilda was too shocked to squawk. She thought she was going to be buried alive.

At last it stopped, but worse was to come. A voice shouted, 'All right, Bill! Up she goes!' and the whole thing began to tip up.

This helped at first, because all the rubbish rolled off Hilda again and unburied her, but it went on tipping until all the rubbish was piled at the other end of the cart, with Hilda, fluttering and furious, tumbled on top of it. It was bad enough to have dustbins emptied on her head, but to be turned upside-down as well! It was too much.

Hilda spread her wings and fluttered to the open end of the cart, which was now facing up to the sky. Just as she got there, the whole thing began to swing down again. Hilda clung desperately to the tailboard as it plunged to earth. When it stopped, she hopped down and began to run. She did not stop running until she was safely back in the farm lane again. She was shaking all over.

'Oh dear,' she clucked, collapsing into a

sad little heap by the ditch. 'Oh dear, dear!'

When she had rested a little, Hilda shook the dust out of her feathers and had a good wash in the ditch.

She felt a lot better after that.

'Silly me!' she muttered to herself as she pecked away at a patch of treacle on her tail. 'I *would* choose a rubbish cart! Never mind. I'm going to see Auntie's chicks somehow. I'll try again tomorrow – on something cleaner!'

And brave little Hilda cocked her head and set off home to the farm.

Hilda gets a lift

The sun was shining brightly when Hilda woke up next morning.

I'm sure I shall find something to take me to Much Wallop today, she thought.

She set out straight after breakfast, looking very important. Anyone could see that she was a hen who was *going* somewhere.

She went down the farm lane and along the main road towards Much Wallop. Right through the village of Little Dollop she went, and past the few cottages on the other side, but she saw nothing she might ride on – except an old doll's pram in somebody's front garden, and that was not much good without somebody to push it.

Then she saw the very thing! It was big and red, shining in the sun – and the driver was just getting into it. There was no time to dither. One thing was certain – it was not a dust cart, and after her terrible experience of the day before, that was all that mattered to Hilda.

She would ride on this.

The extraordinary thing was that a lot of other people seemed to have the same idea! Several men jumped on to it at the same time as Hilda – men with shiny helmets. Hilda had no time to wonder why. She was too busy hanging on. The fire-engine – for that is what it was – had set off at a terrific speed. Hilda was sure she would fall off. She closed her eyes tightly as she was joggled and rattled about and the wind whistled through her feathers. The big silver bell winking in the sun above her head began to clang and clang.

It was all very exciting, and Hilda began to enjoy it. She opened her eyes and looked around her. There was a ladder just above her. She could perch more securely on that. She scrambled up to it and hopped right to the top. She had a splendid view from up there – she could see for miles.

Everything scattered in their path – carts, dogs and bicycles rushed for the shelter of the hedge when they saw, and heard, the fire-engine approaching.

Hilda was delighted. They would soon be at Much Wallop at this rate.

Then she saw to her horror that they were turning off down a side road. This was no good – she would have to get off.

'Stop!' she squawked. 'Stop! I want to get off!' But of course nobody heard her above the noise of the bell.

Then they did stop – suddenly. Hilda was nearly jerked off her perch on the top of the ladder. And the ladder began to move.

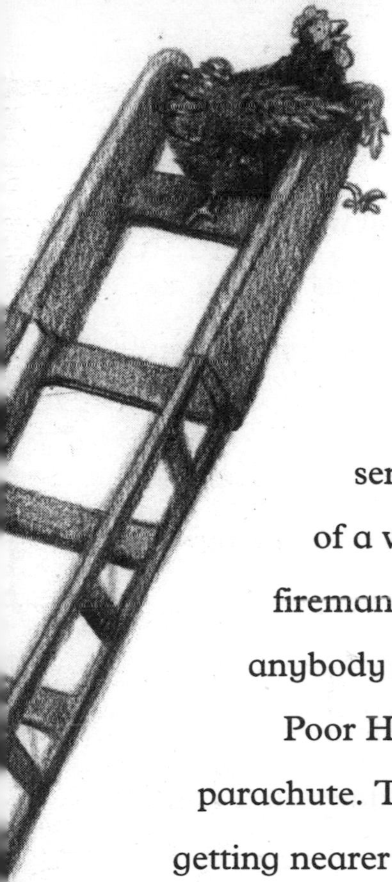

Before Hilda realised what was happening, she was going up and up into the air. They had reached the fire, and the ladder was being sent up to the top windows of a very tall house so that a fireman could climb up and rescue anybody trapped on the top floor. Poor Hilda wished she had a parachute. The smoking windows were getting nearer and nearer and she did not want to be a cooked chicken!

Then the ladder came to rest against the side of the house, and Hilda was relieved to find that she was not to be tipped right into the fire. She heard someone coming up the ladder behind her, and was just going to look round when – whoosh! – a column of water hit the wall beside her and she was drenched.

'Oy!' shouted a voice behind. 'Watch what you're doing with the hoses down there! It's not my bath night!'

Then the fireman saw Hilda – a little huddle of wet feathers hunched at the top of the ladder.

'Hello!' he said. 'What are you doing up here, young lady? You don't look much of a fireman to me! I'll have you down in a jiffy. Just hang on while I have a look round.'

The fireman climbed over her and disappeared over the window-sill into the smoke.

He was soon back again, to Hilda's relief.

'Nobody there, my love. Come on, down we go.'

He took off his helmet and gently lifted Hilda off her perch and placed her in it. She settled down gratefully and had a comfortable ride back to earth again.

It was really awfully kind of him, particularly as she was so wet. Hilda said 'Thank you' in the only way she knew – she laid a nice brown egg in his helmet!

He felt it there when he put in his hand to lift her out.

'Well, I'm blessed!' he said, drawing it out. 'Thank you, love. That'll do fine for my tea.'

'What have you got there?' asked another fireman, coming over to look. The fire was out, and the firemen were getting back on the engine to go home. 'Good heavens! It's Hilda – from Biddick's Farm over Little Dollop way. We'd better take her home.'

So Hilda had another ride on the fire-engine – but sedately this time, in the kind fireman's helmet. He dried her as best he could with his hanky, and let the sun do the rest.

All the other firemen were jealous about the egg.

'Come on, Hilda. Lay one for us,' they teased her.

But Hilda pretended not to notice.

When they got to Little Dollop, Hilda's fireman set her down at the farm gate. She gently pecked his hand to say goodbye and then squeezed under the gate and strutted into the yard. She had created quite a sensation. It isn't every day that a hen arrives home in a fire-engine! All her friends goggled.

It was only when she had told them *all* about it that Hilda realised that her adventures were not over. She still had not seen her auntie's new chicks at Much Wallop.

She would try again tomorrow.

Hilda has a sticky time

Hilda's friends in the farmyard took a great interest in her at breakfast time.

'That's right, Hilda. Have a good breakfast,' said Flo, the oldest hen in the farmyard. 'You'll need to keep your pecker up!'

'You can have some of my grain if you like,' offered a little pullet shyly. 'I can't eat any more.'

'It's all right, thank you, Mary,' said

Hilda. 'I couldn't eat any more myself. Well, I must be going.' She fluffed out her feathers and started towards the gate.

'Can I come with you? Please, Hilda?' begged Mary, hopping along beside her.

'No, Mary. It's too far for you, and anyway it's difficult enough just looking after myself! I'll tell you about it when I come back. Goodbye.'

Hilda squeezed under the gate and set off down the lane.

The others crowded round the gate and watched her go.

'Good luck, Hilda,' they called. 'Give our love to your auntie!'

'I will,' Hilda called back. It was nice of them to see her off like that. She felt very happy and hopeful this morning.

Half an hour later she did not feel anything of the kind. She had walked right through the village and past the place where the fire-engine had been the day before, but still – no lift.

But as she came towards the next bend in the road, Hilda lifted her head and sniffed. There was a strong, hot smell in the air. She rather liked it. When she rounded the corner, she forgot about the smell. There was something moving slowly along by the edge of the road, something that she could ride on.

Hilda had never seen anything quite like it before.

It was rather like a tractor, and it had a

huge roller at the front and a little chimney at the top with dirty smoke coming out of it. It was moving very slowly, but after her feather-raising ride on the fire-engine, this seemed to Hilda to be no bad thing. She hopped up.

The driver saw her.

'Hey! What do you want? Shoo!' he shouted.

Hilda pretended to be deaf. She stayed perched on the roof as if she had grown there.

'All right, stay there, you cheeky little bird. I'll take you home for my lunch. You'll do very nicely with a bit of stuffing.' The driver chuckled and turned back to his wheel.

Hilda felt a little alarmed at this, but she did not move. The man had a nice kindly red face; she was sure he did not really mean it.

Well, almost sure! What was important was to get to Much Wallop.

It was going to take a long time, though. Hilda had not known that anything could move as slowly as this. She could have walked faster, only her feet were so tired. Still, she would have a little rest. She closed her eyes and dozed off.

When she opened her eyes they were going the wrong way! Suddenly Hilda realised what was happening. They were going up and down over the same bit of road!

'Oh, silly me!' clucked Hilda. 'That's what the roller must be for; it's for spreading and flattening the tar to mend the road! Well, I shan't waste any more time here. I shall have to find another lift.'

She went to the back of the roof and

jumped straight down into the road.

Then the terrible thing happened. Hilda could not move! Her feet were stuck! She wriggled and tugged, but it was no good. She was stuck fast in the wet tar.

She started to peck at the tar around her feet to see if she could free them. This was a silly thing to do, as she soon realised. Her beak became stuck together with tar! The steamroller had turned round and was coming back, and she could not open her beak to warn the driver that she was there. She could not manage the tiniest squawk, and the giant roller was coming nearer and nearer. Would the driver see her?

Hilda began to flap her wings to try to attract his attention. If he did not see her – well, he would get his chicken dinner after all, and Hilda was sure he would be sorry.

He did see her. He stopped the roller and climbed down, stepping carefully along the edge of the tar.

'Well, you've got yourself into a fine pickle, haven't you?' he said, looking down at her.

Hilda hung her head in shame.

'I dunno. Some birds!' he said, shaking his head. 'Well, I'll have to get you out somehow. Wait a mo'!'

He stumped off to the roller and came back with a trowel. 'I'll have to dig you out,'

he said, 'and a fine mess that will make of my lovely flat road. You don't deserve to be rescued, my lady.'

Hilda kept very still while he eased the trowel round her feet and prised them out of the tar.

Her claws were all stuck up with it.

'Cor, you are a mess! There's only one thing to do with you.' He lifted her up gently, and carried her back to the roller. He tucked her under his arm while he poured some paraffin from a big can into his baccy tin and set it on the step.

'There now,' he said, standing Hilda in it. 'You stand in that for a while. That should do the trick. Now let's look at this beak. Hmm. You'd better dip that in, too. It won't taste very nice, but it's the best way.'

Hilda looked down at the paraffin round her ankles and shuddered. Then, brave little bird that she was, she shut her eyes, bent down, and plunged her beak into the tobacco tin.

'There's a good girl,' said the driver with admiration. 'That's enough now. Let's see.'

He took Hilda's beak in his hands and gently pulled it apart. Then he rubbed it with a paraffin rag until it was quite free from tar. Hilda clucked quietly in her throat.

The driver lifted Hilda on to his lap and dried her feet thoroughly.

'There you are, you troublesome little baggage. You'd better run along home before I change my mind about that chicken dinner. Go on! Shoo!'

He set her down and shooed her back along the road to Little Dollop. Then he took a trowelful of tar and went back to fill in the holes that Hilda's feet had made in the new road.

When he was safely out of the way, Hilda crept back. He had been very nice to her and she wanted to leave him a present. That done, she set off home.

When the driver came back, he found a nice brown egg beside his baccy tin.

'Well, there's a thing!' he said, looking down the road after her. 'Thank you, little lady.'

The little lady was teased dreadfully when she got home.

'Back already, Hilda? That was a short visit!'

'Oooh, Hilda! You smell awful! Go and have a bath in the horse trough, for goodness' sake!'

Hilda did have a bath in the horse trough, but paraffin is a very *clingy* sort of smell and the others went on being very rude.

'Never mind,' said little Mary consolingly. 'It'll soon wear off.'

'Yes,' said Hilda. 'And you know, there's one good thing about it. I am learning what *not* to get a lift on, and that's very useful.'

Hilda goes out to tea

All the farmyard came to see Hilda off again next day. They teased her a bit, but she did not mind. She squeezed under the gate and turned to say goodbye.

'You be careful now, my girl,' said old Flo. 'Watch where you're putting your feet.'

'And do try not to choose anything smelly,' pleaded Clarissa.

'You wait – I shall smell *lovely* this time,'

said Hilda. 'Goodbye now.'

'Goodbye, Hilda. Good luck!' they called after her.

Hilda *was* luckier this morning. At least she thought she was. There was something parked outside the very first row of cottages. It was a little red and white motor scooter. It was very small, but it had a double saddle, and there would be room for Hilda on that. Under the saddle was a big card with 'L' written on it, but Hilda did not know what that meant.

The proud owner came out of one of the cottages at that moment. It was Miss Smith, the teacher from Little Dollop school. She was wearing an enormous crash helmet. She sat gingerly on the saddle and began to kick at the starter.

Hilda, who had hidden by the hedge until Miss Smith was safely mounted, now crept forward and hopped up on to the saddle. Miss Smith was much too busy to notice her. This was the very first time she had taken the scooter on the road. She had practised a bit in the garden and that was about all.

She kicked the starter a little harder and suddenly the engine burst into life. The scooter made two leaps forward like a learner kangaroo, and then shot off in a cloud of smoke with Miss Smith – and Hilda – hanging on for dear life. In fact, it would be hard to say who was the more frightened – Hilda or Miss Smith herself!

Miss Smith was finding it very difficult to steer. They zigzagged along, one minute careering down the middle of the road, the next heading straight for the ditch. Hilda closed her eyes – she could not bear to look.

They also wobbled. Poor Miss Smith. The more she wobbled, the more she zigzagged, and the more she zigzagged, the more she wobbled.

For Hilda it was like being in a small boat on a rough sea. She began to feel sea-sick.

Round the next bend was a bumpy bit of road. They began to bounce. It was too much for Hilda. At the second bounce she opened her beak and let out a loud squawk!

That was too much for Miss Smith. What was crouching behind her? She wobbled violently, lost control, and drove straight through the hedge.

Luckily they were passing Journey's End Farm at the time, and their journey ended in the middle of a haystack!

When Hilda picked herself up, she felt a bit giddy and stupid and she still had her eyes tight shut. When she realised that at last she was on firm ground again – no more joggling and bouncing – she felt brave enough to open her eyes.

There was a strange mushroom thing

wriggling on the ground by the fallen scooter.

It was poor Miss Smith! Her helmet was jammed right down to her chin and she was wrestling with it to get it off.

Hilda thought that this might be a good moment to disappear. She had tiptoed away only a few yards when, with a sound like a popping cork, Miss Smith emerged from her helmet. She saw Hilda.

'A hen!' she gasped. 'Only a hen! Oh, you did frighten me! Come here! You ought to be ashamed of yourself. What were you doing on my scooter?'

Hilda hung her head. Her feathers were still all ruffled, and bits of hay and chaff were stuck all over her.

Miss Smith looked down at herself. She was just as bad.

'Well, don't just stand there,' she said. 'We must help each other to tidy up.'

So Hilda, who had decided that Miss Smith's bark was worse than her bite, came over and started to peck the bits of straw from Miss Smith's jumper, while Miss Smith picked Hilda's feathers clean. As they worked, Miss Smith gave Hilda a lecture.

'Now, Miss Hen – I hope you've learned your lesson. Never take a ride on something without *asking* first. If I had known you were there, this accident would never have happened. If you want somebody to give you a lift, you must stand by the road and hold your claw up, like this.'

Miss Smith held up her fist and pointed her thumb down the road. 'You see? It's called hitch-hiking, and all drivers understand it. You point your thumb – all right, claw – in the direction in which you want to go, and then if the driver has the time, he will stop and pick you up. You understand?'

Hilda nodded. If only she had known before! Tomorrow she would try it.

'Well,' said Miss Smith, standing up and brushing down her skirt, 'I think we'll do now. My scooter seems to be all right. I'll give you a lift home if you like.'

Hilda didn't like! She was not going through all that again. She backed away.

'It's all right,' said Miss Smith, laughing. 'I think I've had enough for one day, too. I shall *push* it home.'

That was different. Hilda waited while Miss Smith righted the scooter and then she hopped up on the back again. They had a pleasant journey home. Hilda liked Miss Smith.

When they reached her cottage, Miss Smith propped her scooter against the fence.

'Here we are,' she said. 'Oh, I'm dying for a cup of tea.'

Hilda hopped down and looked hopefully at Miss Smith.

Miss Smith was a very understanding person. 'You must be thirsty, too, Miss Hen. Would you care to join me for a cup of tea?'

Hilda had never been invited out to tea before. She followed Miss Smith into her kitchen. Miss Smith put the kettle on and then looked down at Hilda.

'I don't expect tea is much good to you, is it? Let me see what I can find.'

Hilda liked what she found. Miss Smith brought her a cup of water, some porridge oats, and – how could Miss Smith have known? – some cornflakes.

Hilda decided she liked going out to tea.

'Well, you're a very tidy eater, I must say,' said Miss Smith, looking at her clean kitchen floor when Hilda had finished. She hadn't left a crumb. 'You must come again one day.'

Miss Smith saw Hilda to the door. 'I hope you know your way home from here, Miss Hen. Well, goodbye. Remember what I told you – *ask* next time. Goodbye.'

Hilda went down the path and out of the front gate. She paused for a few minutes to leave something for Miss Smith in her upturned crash helmet, and then made for Little Dollop and the farm.

When she reached the gate, everyone rushed to welcome her.

'Hilda! Did you get to Much Wallop?'

'No, I'm afraid not. But I've been to tea with Miss Smith the school teacher.'

'You *haven't*!' They couldn't believe it. Hilda told them all about it.

Then old Flo came up and sniffed her.

'Well, I never! She smells lovely! Come and smell her, girls.' They gathered round and sniffed cautiously.

Hilda smelled faintly of Miss Smith's lavender water.

'I told you I would come home smelling nice,' she said.

Hilda goes hitch-hiking

The following morning, Hilda preened her feathers with special care. She was going to hitch-hike properly today, and she was sure no driver would stop for a *scruffy* hen.

She was just putting the finishing touches to her tail, when Clarissa burst into the henhouse, flapping her wings with a lot of fuss and shaking her untidy head. She looked across at Hilda.

'Well, you're wasting your time,' she said. 'It's raining.'

Hilda quietly went on working at her tail.

'Did you hear what I said?' demanded Clarissa. 'It's pouring with rain. Half the yard is flooded. You'll have mud up to your wish-bone by the time you reach the gate!'

Hilda shuddered. Clarissa did use such vulgar expressions!

'I can at least start out looking respectable,' she said, 'and my feathers will be far more waterproof if they're properly arranged.'

'You're just a fusspot,' said Clarissa.

Hilda cocked a bright eye at her. She was tempted to say something about moth-eaten old boilers, but she sensibly kept it back.

When Hilda was ready, she stepped out of the henhouse door. Clarissa was right about the rain; it was a very wet day indeed. Hilda picked her way carefully across the yard, trying to avoid the puddles.

There was nobody to see her off today except a few ducks, and they were much too busy enjoying themselves to take much notice of her. One gentleman duck did bow to her as she went past, and said, 'Lovely day, what?' but that was all.

When she reached the road, Hilda stationed herself under a large tree which gave her some shelter from the rain, and practised thumbing a lift. It was really quite difficult to balance on one claw and gesture with the other. She fell over several times before she got it right.

She tried it on a green sports car at first, but the driver did not even see her.

I wish I were white, she thought. Speckly brown isn't a very showing-up sort of colour.

After two more cars had gone straight past without stopping or even slowing down, Hilda began to feel a bit hopeless. Who was going to bother to stop and pick up a small soggy hen in this weather?

But somebody did. Just when Hilda was almost ready to give up, she saw a lorry coming. She decided to have one last try. The lorry was not going very fast, and as it came nearer, Hilda got ready. As it drew abreast of her, she fluttered up on to the bonnet and perched there on one claw, hopefully waggling the other one in the direction of Much Wallop.

The driver peered unbelievingly through the windscreen-wipers. A hitch-hiking hen! He had occasionally given lifts to husky young men with shorts and rucksacks – but a *hen*!

He stopped the lorry, slammed down the window and poked his head out into the rain.

'Well, hello there! D'you want a lift to Much Wallop? Come on then – you'd better come in before you're washed away.'

Hilda was so relieved. She hopped on to the enormous hand the young man had thrust out for her, and allowed herself to be drawn inside the cab.

'My, you are wet!' he said kindly, setting Hilda down beside him on the seat. 'I'll put the heater on for a bit.'

He closed the window and turned a knob on the dashboard. They started off and soon there was a comforting wave of warm air filling the cab. After a few minutes Hilda was steaming like a little engine.

'Well, this is very nice,' the young man said. 'I like a bit of company when I'm driving. It stops me going to sleep.'

They drove on for a little while.

Hilda began to get a bit worried. They must be nearing Much Wallop now. Her auntie's farm was just this side of the village, and she did not know how to tell the young man where she wanted to get off.

She hopped on to his lap and jiggled up and down, peering out of the window and clucking gently.

'What's this, then?' said the young man. 'You want to tell me where I'm to put you down, is that it? Well, you squawk good and loud when we get there, and I'll stop for you. All right?'

Hilda nodded. She watched for the two white posts outside Auntie's farm.

There they were! Hilda squawked.

The young man pulled up so sharply that he nearly shot Hilda through the windscreen.

'There you are. How about that for service? It's stopped raining for you, too.

Mind how you go, now.'

The young man opened the door and helped Hilda down the step.

'Wait a minute, though – how are you going to get home?'

Hilda cocked her head on one side and looked hopefully up at him.

'You want me to take you home, do you?' chuckled the young man. 'I dunno – these modern hens! Well, as it happens, I shall be passing about tea-time. If you're waiting for me here, by the posts, at five o'clock, I'll pick you up. All right? Bye-bye, then. Be seeing you.' He slammed the door and the lorry rumbled off.

Hilda looked across at the farm and sighed with happiness. She was here at last!

She looked carefully both ways and

crossed the road. There was a little group of hens just by the gate.

'Er – excuse me,' Hilda said. 'I'm looking for my aunt – a Mrs Emma Hen.'

'Oh, you'll find her in the field over there with her new family,' said one of the hens. 'Just through that white fence.' She pointed to a field with a lot of white coops dotted about.

Hilda thanked her and hurried excitedly across. She squeezed under the fence and looked about her. Which of the coops was Auntie's? There were so many of them, all exactly alike.

Just at that moment, the farmer's little girl began to go down the rows of coops, letting out the hens for their morning exercise. In a few minutes the field was full of proud mothers with their families in tow, like fat kites with long yellow tails jerking in the wind. Each family of little chicks lined up one behind the other after their mother, and wherever she went, no matter how many times she changed direction, they followed in scuttling procession.

Hilda was just wondering how she would find Auntie among all these hens, when one kite broke away from the rest and came rushing to meet her.

'Hilda! How lovely to see you!'

It was Aunt Emma, and behind her tumbled one, two, three, four, five little pom-poms, all cheeping hard.

Well, Hilda *was* glad that she had come. There were no chicks on Biddick's Farm; Mary was the youngest, and she was a pullet – a sort of teenager hen. Hilda had never seen chicks at close hand before, and she loved them. Chicks were fun.

They thought Hilda was fun, too! She played all sorts of games with them. Their favourite was a chasing game. Their mother had to run about with the chicks streaming behind her, twisting and dodging, while the 'fox' – Hilda – tried to catch the littlest one at the end of the line. The chicks 'cheeeeeeeeped!' with excitement as Hilda chased them and pounced again and again. She always missed – until the littlest one began to get caught on purpose.

Then Auntie, who hadn't any breath left, suggested a nice *quiet* game. So they played

Follow My Leader while their mother had a nice rest.

And when they were tired out, the chicks demanded a story. So Hilda settled them around her and told them all about her week's adventures. She told them about the dust cart, and the fire-engine, and the steamroller, and Miss Smith's scooter and the lorry . . .

'Goodness!' she said when she got to that bit. 'That young man said he would pick me up at about five! I must fly.'

'Oh, not yet! Tell us another story, Hilda, *please* tell us another story,' begged the chicks.

'You're a great success,' said Auntie, as they all saw Hilda to the fence. 'It's the first peaceful afternoon I've had since they hatched. Please come and see us again.'

'Yes, please do, please do,' chanted the chicks, bobbing up and down.

'Well, I'll do my best,' Hilda said, 'but you know how it is. I did have a *little* difficulty getting here this time!'

Hilda goes broody

Hilda *had* loved those chicks. For days after visiting them she could think and talk about nothing else.

'They were so sweet,' she told the henhouse for what must have been the hundredth time, 'so soft and fluffy and cuddly. Oh, they were *adorable*.'

Everybody went on scratching – which is rather rude when someone is speaking.

The other hens were just a little tired of Auntie's chicks.

Hilda sighed and wandered out into the yard. She scratched half-heartedly at a bit of chaff, but she was not really interested. Chicks – little yellow chicks – that was all she could think about.

She fluffed out her feathers and tried to imagine what it would feel like to have lots of downy babies jostling under her wings.

Oh, it would be nice to have a family of her very own.

She wandered down the lane at the back of the farm. She had not been there for quite some time, and was surprised to see two little white lambs bouncing all over the meadow at the bottom.

Their mother, Sophie, came over to the

fence to speak to her.

'Good morning, Hilda,' she said. 'You haven't met my family yet, have you? This is Plain and this is Purl.'

'Baa-aa-aa!' said Plain and Purl together, stopping their dance for an instant. Then they were off again, catkin tails a-waggle.

'They're charming,' said Hilda wistfully. She gave a big sigh.

'Why Hilda, whatever's the matter?' asked Sophie kindly. 'You don't seem a bit yourself this morning.'

'I'm not,' Hilda said miserably. 'I feel most peculiar. I've gone off my food and I feel all droopy – and all I can think about is chicks.'

'Is that all!' laughed Sophie. 'Well, that's easily cured. You're just broody, that's all.'

'Broody?' Hilda said.

'Yes. It's very common in hens. What you need is – excuse me . . .'

Sophie turned on the twins who were bouncing round her in the most irritating way. 'For goodness' sake! Either stay up or stay down!'

She turned back to Hilda. 'I'm so sorry. They make me quite dizzy. What was I saying? Oh yes. What you need is a family of your own.'

'Well, I know *that*,' Hilda said peevishly.

'Then instead of brooding about it, why don't you?'

'Why don't I what?'

'Have a family, you silly goose – I mean hen!'

Hilda lifted her head and looked at Sophie.

'Oh, silly, silly me!' she said. 'Of course! That's what I'll do. Thank you, Sophie.'

So next morning Hilda began her family.

It was a small beginning: just a little brown egg at the bottom of her nesting-box. She laid one like it every day.

But today, instead of going off to the

yard with the others to have breakfast, she stayed behind in the henhouse to look after the egg. She settled herself down on it, spreading her soft under-feathers over it carefully. She must keep it warm if it was to hatch out into her first chick.

She sat with her eyes closed, planning how she could lay one every day until she had five or six to hatch.

Mrs Biddick, the farmer's wife, found her there when she came to collect the eggs.

'Hilda? Don't you want any breakfast, you silly bird?' Mrs Biddick thought all hens were silly – even Hilda!

Hilda sat tight.

'Hilda! Come on. Get up, you lazy old thing. I want your egg.'

Hilda knew she did; that's why she wasn't

moving! Mrs Biddick was not going to have *this* egg.

'Oh, Hilda, you haven't gone broody on me. If there's one thing I cannot abide, it's a broody hen. Come on now – hand over!'

Hilda fluffed out her feathers and looked as fierce as she could.

Now it wasn't the first time Mrs Biddick had had to deal with a broody hen. She turned her back on Hilda as if she had given up and busied herself collecting the eggs from the other nesting-boxes.

Hilda relaxed again and continued with her dream. Yes – five or six would make a nice little family.

But before Hilda realised what was happening, Mrs Biddick had turned again, thrust a swift, practised hand under her and taken the precious egg. There it was, lying on top of all those *ordinary* eggs in Mrs Biddick's basket.

'I'm very sorry, Hilda,' said Mrs Biddick as she went towards the door. 'You're one of my best layers. I just can't afford to let you sit.'

Hilda wasn't listening. Her eyes were on that egg on top of the basket. She was not going to let it out of her sight.

She hopped down from her box and followed Mrs Biddick at a safe distance.

Follow that egg!

Mrs Biddick took the basket of eggs straight across the yard and handed it to Mr Biddick, who was loading the milk truck outside the dairy. The Biddicks had a small milk round and supplied milk and eggs to most of Little Dollop.

'Thank you, m'dear,' said Mr Biddick, taking the basket and wedging it carefully between two big churns at the back of the truck. 'How many today?'

'Only twenty-three,' Mrs Biddick said, 'and now it looks as though Hilda's going broody.'

'Aye – she's been a bit restless lately.'

Hilda was more than a bit restless – she was frantic! The egg must be getting *so* cold, exposed to the air like that. She hopped up and down anxiously behind the truck, and as soon as Mrs Biddick had gone back to the house and her husband had his back turned, Hilda jumped up into the truck and crouched behind a big churn. Mr Biddick brought out the last churn, fastened the tailboard and went round to the driving cab.

Before he even had the engine running, Hilda was on that basket. It wasn't very comfortable; twenty-three eggs are a lot of eggs for one small hen. In the end she concentrated upon keeping *her* egg warm –

and on keeping her balance! The truck bounced her up and down like a tennis-ball.

Mr Biddick pulled up outside the first row of cottages in Little Dollop, and came round to the back to get ready to serve. Hilda slithered off her lumpy couch and retreated behind her churn.

Mr Biddick's customers came out to the truck carrying jugs for their milk and basins for their eggs.

'Nice morning, Mr Biddick!' said the first customer. 'I'll have my usual half-pint, please.'

Hilda knew that voice. She peeped out. Yes, it was her friend Miss Smith! She watched as Mr Biddick plunged his long-handled measuring dipper into the churn and poured half a pint of fresh, new milk into Miss Smith's jug.

'Oh, and two eggs, please,' added Miss Smith.

Mr Biddick's large hand descended upon the basket of eggs. Hilda shut her eyes. She knew what was going to happen.

She was right. When she opened her eyes again, her egg was gone. Mr Biddick had put it into Miss Smith's basin!

It was a nice basin, with blue and white stripes, but that was no comfort to Hilda seeing that her family was being carried off in it.

Still, at least she knew where it was going. She could follow it to Miss Smith's as soon as she could get away from the truck without being seen.

At last everybody had been served. Mr Biddick put up the tailboard and prepared to drive off. Hilda slipped down from the truck and scuttled into the hedge. As the back of the truck disappeared down the road, Hilda flew up Miss Smith's path.

The back door was shut. So was the kitchen window, but it had a fairly wide sill. Hilda stood back, took a little run, and jumped up to it. Then she tapped urgently on the window with her beak.

Miss Smith jumped. She had been baking, and she was scraping the mixing bowl with a wooden spoon and having a very undignified lick. She was quite relieved to see that it was only Hilda at the window.

'Why – it's Miss Hen. Do come in.' Miss Smith threw open the window.

It opened outwards, and Hilda was knocked flying! Miss Smith hurriedly opened the door – and promptly sat on the mat with a bump as Hilda dived between her legs and knocked them from under her.

'Help!' cried Miss Smith. 'What on earth is the matter?'

Hilda was rushing wildly round the kitchen with rolling eyes. *Where was that basin?*'

Ah – there it was, on the table. She jumped up, knocking over the flour bin as she did so, and scrambled awkwardly on to the basin. At last! She was with her family again. She settled herself as comfortably as she could.

Miss Smith shook the flour out of her eyes and looked at Hilda, plomped on the basin like a lopsided tea-cosy.

'Have you finished?' she asked acidly. 'Is it safe to get up now?'

Hilda just blinked happily.

Miss Smith picked herself up and cleared away the mess. Then she put on the kettle for a cup of tea. She felt she needed it.

She looked across at Hilda.

'Miss Hen – would you mind telling me

what's so special about that basin? It's empty, you know.'

Hilda looked up at her in horror. She backed awkwardly off the basin and looked into it. There was nothing there at all.

Well, where was the egg then? She began to run round the table, searching for it.

Suddenly Miss Smith understood.

'Oh, Miss Hen! Was one of those eggs yours? Was it very special?'

Hilda took her head out of the sugar packet and looked at Miss Smith.

'Oh dear! What have I done?' Miss Smith felt like a murderer. 'I'm afraid it's in – there.' She pointed to the oven door. A delicious smell had been filling the kitchen for some time.

'I've put your egg into a – into a Victoria sponge!'

Hilda couldn't believe it. She sank on to the table like last year's hat.

Miss Smith looked round wildly for some way of comforting her.

'Oh dear. Er – have some cornflakes!' She grabbed a packet of cornflakes from the dresser and poured a small mountain of them at Hilda's feet.

Hilda looked pained. Cornflakes! At a time like this.

Still – she had not had any breakfast. Perhaps just one or two . . .

As the mountain went down, Hilda's spirits went up. All was not lost. She could lay another egg tomorrow. And this time she would make sure that Mrs Biddick didn't find it!

By the time the mountain had disappeared, Hilda was her perky self again.

Nevertheless, Miss Smith thought it best to see Hilda out of the front door before taking the sponge out of the oven.

It was a beautiful sponge, but poor Miss Smith could not bring herself to eat it. She would have felt like a cannibal.

She gave it to the vicar for the Brownie fête.

The burglar

Hilda had a terrible time trying to find a secret place in which to have her family. Again and again she was discovered and her eggs were taken away.

Mind you, Hilda chose some very silly places: the dog-kennel for instance. She might have known that Old Bailey wouldn't put up with that for long. It was not a very big kennel and Bailey was a very big dog.

He didn't *want* a lodger.

Hilda was pushed out, egg and all. Mrs Biddick spotted it from the kitchen door – and that was the end of that one.

Then there was the old cap of Mr Biddick's that Hilda found on a shelf in a dark corner of the barn. It was very warm and comfortable, and Mr Biddick did not wear it often, but he *did* wear it when it rained.

And one morning when Hilda had to leave her family for a few minutes to pop out for a snack – she had to eat sometimes – it began to rain. Mr Biddick, his mind on pigs and sheep and such (he was going to market) came in hurriedly and slapped the cap on his head.

It only had two eggs in it, but he was not very pleased. Egg shampoos are all very well, but not at nine o'clock in the morning on market day!

The pig trough was not a very bright choice, either. You can't expect pigs to stop eating for three weeks just to oblige a broody hen. In any case, Mr Biddick came along every morning and poured a couple of buckets of pig swill into it.

Horrible stuff, pig swill, with all sorts of nasty things floating in it. Mr Biddick got his own back there all right!

Hilda retired to the hedge to clean up, and then had a good think. Where else could she try? She had tried every possible – and impossible – place in and around the farm buildings.

Of course, there was always the farm-house itself. Hilda had never been inside . . .

That evening Mrs Biddick went to bed before her husband. He was going to have a nice long soak in the bath and do his accounts. He could always do sums best in the bath.

'You go on, m'dear,' he said. 'I'll try not to wake you when I come in.'

Mrs Biddick was tired. She climbed into bed after her hot water bottle and snuggled down. She was almost asleep when she heard the noise.

It was a sort of stirring sound, and it came from under the bed!

Mrs Biddick lay there in the dark, her eyes wide open, listening. There it was again. No doubt about it, there was somebody there.

Mrs Biddick was braver than most of us. She took a deep breath, leaned out and peeped under the bed.

There was an eye looking at her.

Mrs Biddick didn't feel brave any more.

'Help!' she screamed. 'Ben! Ben!'

She made an enormous leap from the bed to the door, fearful that 'it' would grab her leg as she went past, and bumped into something huge and wet and slippery.

'Help!' screamed Mrs Biddick at the top of her voice.

'I *am* helping,' said Mr Biddick. 'Or at least I would be, m'dear, if you would just take your head out of my stomach.'

'Oh Ben! It's you.' Mrs Biddick detached herself from her dripping husband. 'Ben – there's a burglar under the bed.'

'Is that all! You got me out of a perfectly good bath just for a burglar?'

'No, Ben, really. I saw his eyes. I know there's somebody there.'

Mr Biddick sighed, girded up his towel and strode over to the bed.

'Burglar!' he said firmly. 'Come out. I'm sorry, but my wife insists.'

Nothing happened.

Mr Biddick bent down and poked his head underneath the bed.

The burglar looked at Mr Biddick, and Mr Biddick looked at the burglar.

Mr Biddick retreated. 'I'm not putting my hand in there!' he said.

'Why not?' asked Mrs Biddick, wide-eyed. 'What's under there?'

'Well, you never know with burglars. She might peck me.'

'Hilda!' said Mrs Biddick. 'It's that hen, isn't it? That does it. She's going in the pot. In the pot, first thing in the morning. You wait, my girl!' Mrs Biddick looked about for a weapon.

Hilda decided not to wait. She scuttled between Mr Biddick's wet feet, dodged Mrs Biddick's hair-brush, and scooted down the landing. She practically flew down the banisters and into the kitchen. She hid under the table.

Mr Biddick took the hair-brush from Mrs Biddick's trembling hand and made soothing noises.

'There now, my luvver. Easy now. I'll get my dressing-gown on and make you a nice cup of tea.'

He went downstairs and put the kettle on. Very quietly, he opened the back door and let the burglar out.

'Hop it,' he whispered, 'or there'll be chicken soup for dinner tomorrow!'

Hilda hopped.

Mr Biddick was just about to pour out the tea when there was a terrible shriek from upstairs, followed immediately by strange thumps.

Mr Biddick put down the teapot and went upstairs to investigate.

'Not *another* burglar!' he said, putting his head round the door.

It was not another burglar. It was just

that Mrs Biddick had decided to join her husband in the kitchen, and had started to put on her dressing-gown and slippers.

And Hilda had left one of her family in the left slipper, and Mrs Biddick had not noticed it until it was too late.

She was hopping about trying to find somewhere to put her sticky foot. The eggshell was sharp and she couldn't put her foot down, but she couldn't step out of the slipper because of the mess it would make on the carpet.

Mr Biddick was a great help.

'Trust you to put your foot in it, maid,' he said, grinning all over his face.

At that moment Mrs Biddick knew exactly what to do with her eggy slipper.

She was a good shot. Mr Biddick had to get back in the bath.

Hilda is really brave

Next morning Hilda ran away.

She did not really run away – not for good, that is. She intended to come back again when she had hatched out her family.

It was just that she thought it might be a good idea to get out of Mrs Biddick's way for a while! She thought that she might have more chance of keeping her eggs if she laid them away from the farm altogether.

By milking time Hilda was far across the fields, out of sight of the farm. This time she must find a really good place for her nest. She squeezed under gates and hedges, and inspected every ditch.

Hilda knew exactly what she wanted.

It had to be somewhere that was safe from people – like farmers with buckets.

It had to be a place that did not belong to somebody else who might want it back – no more kennels or caps or slippers.

Above all, it had to be where Mrs Biddick could not find it. Even if she did not put Hilda in the pot, she would take away the eggs to sell – and Hilda was determined that *this* family should not end up in a Victoria sponge!

Hilda knew exactly what she needed – and she found it at the end of an old overgrown cart track which looked as if nobody had been down it for years. Grass was growing down the middle, and brambles and nettles pressed in from either side.

And at the end of it, beyond a broken gate, was an old cottage.

There was no door to the cottage. Like the windows, it was just a gaping hole. Much of the roof had fallen in, and the crumbling walls looked as if *they* would fall down if the tall, strong weeds which were holding them up were to let go for a minute. Nobody had lived in it for a very long time and it was unlikely that anybody would ever want to do so again – except, perhaps, a little speckled hen.

Hilda threaded her way through the weeds excitedly and peeped inside.

The cottage was just an empty shell, but

the corner on the left of the doorway was curtained with cobwebs, and propped against the wall was an old mattress. Hilda picked her way across the dusty, rotten floor and looked behind it.

There, black with age but with the handle still firmly attached, was an old frying-pan.

What better place to make her nest? Hilda tried it for size, patting round and round and then settling in it.

It fitted; it might have been made for her. Hilda had found her secret place. Nobody would think of looking for her here.

Hilda shifted uncomfortably in the hard frying-pan. It could do with a bit of padding. Then she looked up at the mattress. Well, that was not going to be very difficult to arrange. She tugged at some loose stuffing with her sharp beak, and soon her new home had a nice warm lining.

Now she was ready to have her family.

By the end of the week, Hilda had laid six eggs. Then she decided to stop. There wasn't really room for more in the frying-pan and she could get them all tucked neatly under her. If she had another, there would always be one left out in the cold.

Now all she had to do was sit – and sit – and sit. It was very boring. And lonely. She longed for a good gossip with someone. She was getting hungry, too. There was really very little for a hen to eat around the cottage, except for a worm or two.

She was sitting there one morning, dreaming of cornflakes – mountains and mountains of cornflakes – when she thought she heard a car.

It was a car. And three lorries, and a bulldozer and an enormous earth-excavator on caterpillar treads. It sounded like a tank as it rumbled past the cottage. It shook the old walls to their foundations even before they began to knock them down.

For that is what they had come to do, the men in the lorries. They were going to knock down Hilda's cottage and level the land around it to make room for twenty new houses.

Of course, all that poor Hilda knew was that once again her family was in danger. She sat frozen behind her mattress screen as boots scrunched on the path, came inside, walked round and went out again. What on earth was going on?

She soon found out. There were bumps

and thumps on the roof. Then came a shattering crash as a hatchet bit into a beam. Then another and another.

They were tearing down the roof.

Hilda was terrified. She wanted to run away, but she could not do that. She couldn't leave her family. She was going to keep *this* family if it killed her.

It nearly did. Soon there were beams crashing down. And slates. And bricks. Only Hilda's mattress saved her. Beams fell across it, slates bounced off it, plaster coated it; it was soon almost buried in dust. But Hilda remained unharmed beneath it – dusty, and very frightened, but unharmed.

Then they began to knock down the walls. The noise was deafening. Hilda felt battered and bludgeoned by it. The floor beneath her shook with every crash. It was like being in an earthquake.

Hilda wanted to run. She wanted to terribly, but she didn't. Being brave isn't not being frightened. It is being frightened and still not running away.

And Hilda was really brave. She sat there guarding her eggs while the walls fell down – and she didn't run.

Then Harry found her.

Harry was supposed to be knocking down Hilda's wall – it was the only one left standing – but he had stopped for a breather. He bent down to tuck a flapping trouser leg in his boot, and saw Hilda's eye gleaming from under the mattress.

Harry thought it must be a cat at first. He moved a beam to take a closer look – and there was Hilda.

Harry could not believe his eyes. He called his foreman.

'Here, George! Come and see what I've found!'

George scrambled over the rubble and peered behind the mattress.

'Crikey!' he said. 'A hen. D'you mean to say she's been sitting here through all this?' He waved his arm at the wreckage.

'She must have been, poor little blighter. Deserves a medal, that's what she does. She must be sitting – wouldn't leave her eggs.'

'Well, she can't stay here. They'll be coming to clear this lot in a minute.'

Harry looked down at brave little Hilda.

'Look, George – couldn't we leave her – just until her eggs hatch out? I mean, after all she's been through . . .'

'Oh, come off it, Harry. We can't hold up a whole housing scheme just for a hen. Families have been waiting for these houses for months.'

'Well, what about *her* family? She's done her best for it, hasn't she?'

Hilda liked Harry.

But George had his job to do – and he had noticed something.

'Look, Harry, we don't have to turn her off her nest. Look what she's sitting in! We can move her, family and all. Here, hang on to this mattress!'

George crawled under the mattress and backed out very carefully with the frying-pan and its contents.

Hilda was still very dazed, but she tried to look as dignified as possible.

A voice came from the other side of the wall.

'Isn't anybody doing any work around here? Where's George?'

George hurriedly handed the frying-pan to Harry.

'Here – take it. She's all yours.'

'What shall I do with her?'

'I don't know. You're the one who wanted to give her a medal.' George hurried off.

Harry and Hilda looked at each other.

'I suppose I'll just have to take you home,' said Harry.

Hilda's family

Harry felt pretty silly carrying the frying-pan across the building site – and did his friends laugh!

But this was nothing to what Harry's landlady had to say when he got Hilda home.

'You're not bringing that fowl in here! Just think what she'll do to my clean carpets!'

'But she's sitting,' poor Harry pleaded. 'She's going to have a family.'

'Not in here, she isn't. You know the rules – No Pets Allowed!'

'I could put newspaper down,' Harry said, 'and she could stay in my room . . .'

'No!' said the landlady.

So Harry and the frying-pan and Hilda went down the main street of Little Dollop in search of a home.

And whom should they meet but Miss Smith! She was just coming out of the village shop and she *was* surprised to see Hilda approaching in a frying-pan!

'Hello, Miss Hen! Hitch-hiking again?'

Harry beamed at Miss Smith. 'You know her, Miss? You know who she belongs to?'

'Yes. She comes from Biddick's Farm. Hilda and I are old friends, aren't we, Hilda?'

Hilda clucked in her throat. Miss Smith

looked at Harry.

'The Biddicks have been looking for her everywhere. Where did you find her?'

Harry explained about the building site. 'Deserves a medal, she does,' he finished.

'I think she would most probably prefer some cornflakes,' said Miss Smith. Hilda brightened considerably. 'I had better take her home with me. I shall be seeing Mr Biddick in the morning when he comes with the milk.'

Harry – with relief – handed Hilda over to Miss Smith.

'I hope Mr Biddick will let her keep the eggs,' he said. 'She deserves to, after sticking by them like that.'

'I hope so, too,' said Miss Smith. 'I shall do my best to persuade him.'

So Hilda went home with Miss Smith – to cornflakes, and safety and peace.

Before they settled down for the night, Miss Smith left the back door ajar for a few minutes in case Hilda should feel like stretching her legs. Hilda was longing for a good scratch, but she wasn't very sure about leaving her eggs. She had not quite forgiven Miss Smith for the Victoria sponge! However, Miss Smith promised to look after them *very* carefully, so Hilda popped over the back step and scratched around the little yard. She shook the last of the dust from her feathers before returning to her family.

And before she went to sleep, Miss Smith had a long think about Hilda.

When Mr Biddick came with the milk next morning, Miss Smith asked him in and told him all about Hilda's terrible time in the ruined cottage.

'You will let her hatch the eggs now, won't you, Mr Biddick?' she pleaded.

Mr Biddick rubbed his chin. 'Well, I don't know about that. You see, she's a good little layer, our Hilda, and we can't really afford to let her take time off to rear chicks. They stop laying, you see, that's the trouble.'

Miss Smith made up her mind. 'Mr Biddick, would you consider lending Hilda to me for a while?'

'Lend Hilda to you, Miss Smith? Whatever for?'

'Well, we are just learning about frog spawn and birds' eggs in our Nature class at school. Now if I could *rent* Hilda for a few weeks I could give the children a live lesson –

much better than me trying to draw it on the blackboard.'

'You mean you want to take Hilda to *school*, Miss Smith?'

'Why not? I'm sure Hilda won't mind if it means that she can keep her family. It seems to me to be an excellent plan.'

And that is how Little Dollop School came to have a hen in the classroom – along with three jars of tadpoles and Freddy Hicks' uncle's collection of birds' eggs. Hilda occupied the place of honour in the hole under Miss Smith's desk in front of the class. There she sat in her frying-pan as happy as a queen. Sitting is a boring and lonely business. This was much more fun.

The children thought so too! Hilda became a sort of new girl. They took her out into the playground with them in Break, and shared their elevenses with her (she didn't care for aniseed balls, but popcorn was a different matter). They brought her little presents of worms and rice krispies. They tiptoed about and tried not to shout or bang their desk-lids, so as not to startle her. They had never been so quiet. Miss Smith felt that there was a lot to be said for having a hen in class!

And somehow all the lessons seemed to centre around Hilda. They drew pictures of her for Art. They wrote a composition called 'The hen who came to school' for English. They counted eggs for Arithmetic. They sang 'Please Little Hen' and 'Naughty Little Henny Penny' in the singing lesson. At story time Miss Smith told them about some of Hilda's adventures. These were very popular, particularly the one where Miss Smith and Hilda ended up in a haystack.

In Nature Study they learned about eggs. They learned how the baby chick starts as a tiny speck in the egg, and grows and grows for twenty-one days until it is strong enough to break its way out into the world.

And they all looked at Hilda and wondered when *her* little chicks would begin to break their way out.

One morning when the class was working very quietly making models – of Hilda of course – in plasticine, a little boy in the front row put his hand up.

'I'm sure I can hear tapping, Miss.'

Now this was not unusual. At least a dozen times during the week someone had been sure he or she could hear tapping. But this time when Miss Smith put her ear to the frying-pan, *she* could hear it. She looked up excitedly and spoke to the class.

'Now I want you to come up very quietly and kneel round my desk. No pushing!'

The children came up like little mice and settled around the frying-pan. Hilda was surprised, but pleased to see them. She was completely used to them now.

'Hilda,' Miss Smith said, 'I think your

family is coming. May we have a look?'

Well, of course, Hilda wanted to have a look too, so she raised herself gently off the eggs and stepped back from the frying-pan.

There was an 'Aah!' of disappointment from the children. The eggs looked just the same as usual. Then Miss Smith, asking Hilda for permission, picked up each egg in turn and held it to her ear.

In one of them there was a distinct tapping. She held it for each child to hear, and then put it back carefully with the others.

'Watch!' she whispered.

As they watched, a small crack appeared in the egg, and then a little hole. Now they could see a tiny beak jabbing at the shell from inside. The hole got bigger and bigger – and at last a little damp head squeezed through.

The little chick wriggled and struggled and pushed – until at last it burst the egg right open and fell out.

It didn't move.

'Oh, is it dead?' Jane whispered.

'No, just resting,' said Miss Smith.

Hilda was worried, too. She watched her first chick anxiously. It didn't look right at all – so limp and damp and scrawny. But in a few minutes it was trying out its feet, and as it dried off in the air it began to look as fluffy as a chicken should.

And as cracks appeared in the other eggs and the children began to get very excited, Hilda reached down to welcome her first baby.

She could not quite believe it – until the chick opened its beak and gave its first, strong 'Cheep!'

Then Hilda knew that she had a family of her very own at last.